Sam took a deep breath but he could hear the edge which crept into his voice.

'Are you telling me that you've walked all that way by yourself?'

'How else could I get home?' Holly shrugged but he saw a little colour rise to her cheeks despite her apparent nonchalance. 'Anyway, I'm not a kid, Sam. I *can* look after myself. I've been on my own in worse places than this in the past year, believe me!'

'I don't doubt it.' There was a sting to the words which whipped a bit more colour into her face. Sam wasn't sure why he felt so angry, though. After all, what business was it of his what she did?

Dear Reader

One of the joys of writing is the opportunity it gives you to create new characters, so you can imagine my delight when I was asked to create a whole town!

Yewdale is purely the product of my imagination but during the course of writing this series the characters who live there became very real to me. Gruff old Isaac Shepherd, nosy Marion Rimmer, the Jackson family with their frequent crises... I would sit down at the typewriter each morning, eager to discover what was happening in their lives.

Writing this series has been quite simply a delight. I have had the pleasure of not only bringing together each couple and watching them fall in love, but of seeing how their lives were enriched by the people around them. I hope that you enjoy reading the books as much as I have enjoyed writing them.

My very best wishes to you.

Jennifer Taylor

HOME AT LAST

BY
JENNIFER TAYLOR

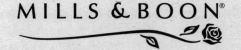

MILLS & BOON®

First published in Great Britain 1999
Harlequin Mills & Boon Limited,
Eton House, 18-24 Paradise Road, Richmond, Surrey TW9 1SR

© Jennifer Taylor 1999

ISBN 0 263 81719 9

Set in Times Roman 10½ on 12 pt.
03-9907-49963-D

Printed and bound in Spain
by Litografia Rosés, S.A., Barcelona

CHAPTER ONE

IT WAS five minutes past midnight when the phone rang. Sam O'Neill groaned as he switched on the bedside lamp. He'd been hoping for a quiet night but it seemed he was doomed to disappointment!

'O'Neill,' he answered crisply, having picked up the receiver.

'It's Harvey Walsh over at Yewthwaite Farm, Dr O'Neill. I'm sorry to bother you but it's Helen, you see. She's had a bit of an accident.'

'What's happened, Harvey?' Sam's dismay at being woken disappeared immediately. Like most of the farmers in the area, Harvey Walsh would never have dreamt of phoning if he hadn't thought it urgent.

'Helen's burnt her arm on the stove. Said she tripped, although I've no idea what she could have fallen over…' Harvey took a deep breath but Sam could hear the anxiety in his voice as he continued. 'Anyway, it looks real bad to me. Can you come and take a look at it, Dr O'Neill?'

'Of course. I'll be there just as soon as I can. In the meantime, try to make Helen as comfortable as possible. If she's wearing any jewellery, a watch or a bracelet perhaps, then take them off in case her arm starts to swell up.'

'Shall I put anything on the burn? I made Helen put her arm in a bowl of cold water straight away, but Mum always used to say that putting butter on a burn would help…'

'No!' Sam cut in quickly. 'That is one old remedy which will do more harm than good. Don't do anything more until I get there. I'll see how bad Helen's arm is and then decide what needs to be done after that.'

Sam wasted no time after he'd hung up. He'd left his clothes over the back of a chair and it took only minutes to slip into the navy chinos and blue check shirt then run his fingers through his tousled black hair. The night was warm so he didn't bother with a jacket as he let himself out of the house and got into his car.

The summer had been marvellous that year, long hot days followed by balmy nights, and that night was no exception. The sky was a deep inky blue above the towering peaks of the mountains that surrounded the small Cumbrian town of Yewdale, where he had been working as a locum for the past year.

He smiled to himself as he quickly left the town behind and headed out into open country. He couldn't believe how fond he'd grown of the place. When he'd accepted the job it had been merely as a stop-gap, a way to fill in time and gain valuable experience before he got on with what he really wanted to do with his life.

His ambition had always been to work overseas once he qualified—in Africa where doctors' skills were needed desperately. The fact that he'd enjoyed his stint here in Cumbria so much had come as a surprise, although it hadn't changed his mind about what he intended to do. Come October he'd be flying out to Mozambique and he felt a stir of excitement as he thought about the challenges ahead, but he had to admit that he'd miss this town and all the friends he'd made here...

The thought came to an abrupt halt as he rounded a bend and a figure loomed into view. Slamming on the brakes, Sam brought the car to a stop with a squeal of tyres. His heart was pounding as he thrust open the door and got out. He'd come within a hair's breadth of running the girl down. Hadn't she more sense than to go wandering down the road like that in the middle of the night?

'What the hell do you think you're doing?' he demanded, then stopped as he got his first really good look at her. In growing disbelief, his gaze flew from the tangle of honey-brown curls to the shapeless red T-shirt and baggy jeans, before coming to rest on the laden rucksack which seemed in imminent danger of forcing her down into the ground by its sheer weight.

'Holly?' he said incredulously. 'It *is* you, isn't it?'

'Don't sound so surprised. Surely I haven't changed that much!' She gave a husky laugh but it only seemed to underline the exhaustion on her face. 'Hello, Sam. I'm sorry if I gave you a fright just now. I didn't hear the car, to be honest. I must be more tired than I realised.'

She glanced back along the road, swaying a little as she turned to face him again. 'The coach driver dropped me off at the motorway service station so that I wouldn't have to go all the way through to Kendal. But I didn't realise how long a walk it was from there.'

'"How long a walk..."' Sam took a deep breath

but he could hear the edge which crept into his voice. 'Are you telling me that you've walked all that way by yourself? It must be a good five miles at least. What on earth were you thinking of, doing such a crazy thing?'

'How else could I get home? There's no bus at this time of the night and I don't have the money for a taxi. I spent every penny I had on the coach fare from London.' She shrugged but he saw a little colour rise to her cheeks despite her apparent nonchalance. 'Anyway, I'm not a kid, Sam. I *can* look after myself. I've been on my own in worse places than this in the past year, believe me!'

'I don't doubt it.' There was a sting to the words which whipped a bit more colour into her face. Sam wasn't sure why he felt so angry, though. After all, what business was it of his what she did?

Holly Ross was the daughter of David Ross, one of the practice's three senior partners. Sam had met her only briefly when he'd started working in Yewdale. Holly had come home from university to see her mother, who'd been seriously ill at the time.

After her mother's death, Holly had dropped out of medical school and taken off, backpacking her way around the world. Although David had said little over the ensuing months, Sam knew that he'd been worried about his eldest daughter. And no wonder. Looking at her now, he couldn't in all honesty say that it appeared the trip had done her good!

His deep brown eyes made another lightning-fast study of her. She looked as though she hadn't had a decent meal in ages, he decided critically. The loose T-shirt certainly didn't disguise the fact that she was painfully thin. Her green eyes looked enormous in her heart-shaped face, the shadows under them lending her a waif-like vulnerability which tugged at his heartstrings.

He had a crazy urge to put his arms around her and tell her that everything was all right now because he'd take care of her. It shook him. One thing he'd steadfastly avoided had been any kind of commitment!

'Does David know that you're coming home tonight?' he asked tersely instead, shocked by his response to her.

'No.' Holly raised those huge green eyes to his so that he could see the uncertainty they held before she quickly looked away. 'I…I thought I'd surprise him.'

'Well, you should do that, all right!' He laughed gruffly, determined not to let her see the effect she'd had on him. He shot a glance along the road, deeming it safer to keep his mind on the problems this encounter had caused.

He was torn between the need to get to Yewthwaite Farm as quickly as possible and a deep reluctance to leave Holly there. It had nothing whatsoever to do with that mental aberration he'd suffered just now, of course—but simple common sense. It was a good three miles to Yewdale even from here so how could he drive off and leave her? Anything could happen to her at this time of the night, and he wasn't prepared to have *that* on his conscience!

'Come along.' He slid his hand under her elbow as he came to a decision, swiftly propelling her to where his car was slewed across the road, its bonnet just an inch away from the ditch.

'You don't have to drive me home!' Holly tried to shake his hand off—a futile attempt to free herself, in his view, seeing as she looked as though a puff of wind would have blown her away. His brows rose, the mockery in his voice once more bringing the colour rushing to her face.

'I'm not.'

'Oh! Then what…? I mean…where are you taking me?' She was obviously nonplussed by his reply, her eyes mirroring her confusion as she stared at him. Sam felt as though his heart had skipped a beat all of a sudden, his lungs missing a vital breath of air as he looked into their luminous depths.

He couldn't recall ever seeing eyes that shade of emerald before or lashes so thick and black that they cast delicate shadows on her cheeks. She wasn't wearing a scrap of make-up, as far as he could tell, yet her skin had a velvety smoothness in the glow from the headlamps which made his fingers itch to touch it. It was only when he felt the tremor of exhaustion that ran through her that he realised he was wasting more time than he had to spare by standing there.

'I'm out on a call at the moment. Helen Walsh over at Yewthwaite Farm has had an accident and burned her arm.' Even as he was speaking Sam was opening the car door. He let go of Holly's arm and reached for her backpack. 'I'll drop you off at home after I've been over there to see her.'

'Oh, I see. But there's no need to go to all that trouble, honestly.' She stubbornly clung to the straps of her rucksack. 'I can manage perfectly well—'

'I'm sure you can.' He smiled tightly, unsure why

he felt so annoyed by her reluctance to accept his help. If the wretched girl wanted her independence that much, why argue? And yet he knew that he wouldn't have a moment's peace thinking about her wandering around alone in the middle of the night. 'However, if anything *did* happen to you I imagine David would blame me for leaving you here. Frankly, I can do without the aggravation. So humour me, please.'

He stared back at her calmly, watching the rapid play of emotions that crossed her face. It was obvious that she was torn between a desire to stick to her guns—especially now that he'd explained his reasons for offering to help her—and reluctance to cause a scene.

He glanced pointedly at his watch and heard her sigh as she shrugged the rucksack off her shoulders and relinquished it to his care. She climbed into the passenger seat without another word, leaving him to toss the bag into the back before he slid behind the wheel.

They drove in silence for a couple of miles, Holly sitting with her face averted as she stared out of the window. It was obvious that she didn't appreciate being coerced into doing what he wanted, but Sam couldn't help that. It was for her own good and it would save *him* spending the rest of the night wondering if she'd made it home safely, although he didn't dwell on why he should be so concerned.

'So, how is Dad, then?'

He started as Holly suddenly broke the silence, feeling a rush of heat flowing through his veins as he turned to look at her. The glow from the dashboard softened the thin planes of her face so that she looked heartbreakingly young and beautiful at that moment. He felt his body stir with a speed that shocked him.

This was David's *daughter*, for heaven's sake! he berated himself. But the rebuke was less of a dampener than it should have been.

'Sam?'

There was a faint uncertainty in her voice now which reminded him that he hadn't answered the question. Sam returned his attention to the road, but he could feel ripples of awareness racing through his system in the most peculiar way. 'He's fine. Working hard as usual, but that goes without saying, I imagine.'

'And Mike and Emily?' Her tone had softened as she'd mentioned her brother and sister. 'I bet Emily has grown a lot while I've been away.'

'She has. Mike, too. You'll be surprised when you see them.' He frowned as a sudden thought struck him. 'Did you know that Emily has been ill?'

'Ill? No. Why? What's wrong with her?'

He heard the panic in her voice and cursed himself for not realising what a shock it might be for her. 'Nothing,' he said quickly. 'She's perfectly fine now. She had meningitis but fortunately it was diagnosed in its very early stages so she made a full recovery.'

'Meningitis!' she echoed in horror. 'But that's awful! I had no idea…'

'How could you?' He reached over and squeezed her hand, wanting to offer some measure of comfort. 'And, as I said, Emily is fine now. She's looking forward to being a bridesmaid at Elizabeth's wedding next month,' he added as an extra reassurance, and saw the startled look Holly shot him.

'Elizabeth is getting married? Really? Who to?'

'James Sinclair, the new partner in the practice.'

'The new partner?' Her face was a picture. 'I had no idea there *was* a new partner!'

'No?' Sam frowned again, surprised that she hadn't heard. 'You know that Elizabeth's father had a heart attack last Christmas and decided to retire?' he asked, then carried on when she nodded. 'Well, Elizabeth and your father decided to advertise for a third partner when it became obvious that the practice was under increasing pressure. They took James on in April.'

He laughed reminiscently. 'It was quite funny at first because Elizabeth was extremely antagonistic towards James, which isn't like her, as you know. However, things worked out better than any of us dared hope, and she and James are getting married at the end of September.'

'But that's wonderful news! Although it is a surprise.' Holly sighed ruefully. 'It's been difficult keeping in touch recently. It wasn't so bad at first because I phoned home fairly regularly. But when my money started to run out I had to be really careful and just send the odd postcard to let everyone know that I was all right.

'I had a couple of letters from Dad while I was in Rio—I managed to find a job there at one of the hotels. But I've been moving round a lot since then so I haven't received any mail for ages now.'

'I see.' Sam put both hands back on the wheel as he turned into the farm road and the car bounced over the bumps. He drew up in front of the house just as the door opened and Harvey Walsh appeared. He gave the man a quick wave then glanced at Holly as he cut the engine.

Obviously there was a lot she didn't know and suddenly he wasn't sure how to handle the situation. Was it his place to tell her what had happened in the past few weeks? Or should he leave it to David to do that? How would she react when she found out that her father had got married again?

'It seems that I *have* missed a lot while I've been away!' Holly unwittingly echoed Sam's thoughts. She glanced towards the farmhouse and sighed as she saw Harvey waiting on the step. 'Still, now isn't the time to catch up on what's been happening around here, is it? It will have to wait till later. I don't want to get in the way, Sam, so I'll stay in the car, if that's all right with you.'

'Of course. It shouldn't take long anyway. I just want to see how bad Helen's arm is and whether or not she'll need to go to hospital.' He reached for his case as he opened the door, relieved that he'd been spared making a decision about what to tell her. He'd become adept at avoiding emotional entanglements, and the thought of getting involved in this situation seemed fraught with danger to him. And yet he couldn't quite bring himself to walk away without a final word of reassurance. 'Sure you'll be OK out here on your own?'

'I'll be fine.' She smiled as she looked towards the darkened hills. 'It's good to be back, Sam. I'm just going to sit here and let it sink in that I'm home at last.'

Sam took a quick breath as he closed the car door but it didn't dispel the tension that knotted his stomach all of a sudden. He couldn't explain it but it felt as though something had changed. Why?

He strode towards the house then paused to glance back, frowning as his gaze alighted on the girl in the car. All that had happened was that Holly Ross had come home, and how could that have any effect on his life? He knew where he was going and what he wanted—every single detail had been mapped out a long time ago. Holly's return couldn't make a scrap of difference to his plans...

'Right, Helen, that should make you feel more comfortable, I imagine.'

Sam finished bandaging Helen Walsh's arm. Although it was obviously a painful injury, in his opinion the burn didn't require hospital treatment. The prompt immersion in cold water had stopped it blistering too badly and he was confident that the skin would heal by itself. The tulle gras dressing he had applied beneath the bandage would minimise any risk of infection.

'Thank you, Dr O'Neill. I feel such a fool, tripping over my own two feet like that...' Helen sighed as she glanced at her husband, who was standing anxiously beside her chair.

'So long as you're all right, love. Although you do seem to be having a lot of little accidents lately.' Harvey patted his wife's shoulder but there was a definite trace of concern in the look he gave Sam. 'Falling against the Aga is just one of a whole list of things which have happened lately, Dr O'Neill. It all started when Helen fell down the stairs a couple of months back and sprained her ankle.'

'That was just one of those things, Harvey!' Helen put in quickly, obviously annoyed that her husband had brought it up. 'You know how steep those stairs are. It's a wonder one of us hasn't tripped on them before!'

'That's as maybe. But how about when you fell over in town last week while you were shopping? You can still see the bruise on your forehead from where you bumped it against the wall,' Harvey replied, glancing at Sam as though seeking his support.

'Maybe you're in too much of a rush to get things done, Helen. You'll have to slow down a bit,' Sam replied lightly, but it did seem odd that she should be having so many accidents all of a sudden.

He closed his case, frowning as he shot her an assessing look. Helen Walsh was a pretty and capable woman in her thirties, who worked hard, helping her husband run the farm which was the biggest in the area. The fact that Harvey's mother, the indomitable old Mrs Walsh, lived with them and was virtually bedridden now must have only increased Helen's workload. Yet he found himself wondering if it was just rushing around which was causing the trouble or something more.

'Apart from these recent episodes, how have you been feeling in general, Helen?' he asked quietly.

'Fine,' she replied a shade too quickly. She avoided Sam's eyes as she plucked the edge of the bandage. 'As you say, Dr O'Neill, I'll just have to take things easy for a change. Next time Harvey suggests a cup of bedtime cocoa I'll send him down to make it!'

They all laughed but Sam couldn't shake off the feeling that Helen wasn't telling him the whole truth, a feeling endorsed by what Harvey said as he saw him to the door.

'I've been worried about Helen for some time now, Doctor, to be honest.' Harvey glanced over his shoulder and lowered his voice so that it wouldn't carry back to the kitchen. 'I can't put my finger on it but there's something not quite right with her.'

'In what way?' Sam frowned. 'Can you be more specific?'

'Well, it's difficult to pin it down… She just doesn't seem herself. I've noticed that she's unsteady on her feet at times. And occasionally her speech sounds sort of slurred. I've tried suggesting that she has a word with you, but she won't hear of it.'

'I know how hard Helen works, especially now your mother needs so much attention. Maybe she's overtired and that's what's causing the trouble,' Sam suggested, although he wasn't convinced that was the answer.

'I suppose so.' Harvey sounded doubtful. 'I'm always telling her to take things easier, not that she takes any notice, mind. But I'd just like to make certain that there isn't anything wrong, you understand.'

'Then have another go at trying to persuade her to come into the surgery. If it's causing you concern then it needs looking into.' Sam smiled reassuringly but it was obvious that Harvey was worried about his wife. 'In the meantime I'll arrange for Abbie Fraser

to come in to change the dressing on Helen's arm.
I'll have a word with Abbie and see if she can talk
Helen into having a check-up, shall I?'

'Would you? I'd appreciate that, Doctor.' Harvey
gratefully accepted the suggestion, making Sam realise how concerned he was.

He went back to the car, thinking about what
Harvey had told him. Was there something wrong
with Helen other than the fact that she had far too
much to do? He would hate to think that he was
opting for the easy answer, rather than trying to find
out what the real problem was, but it was going to
be difficult if Helen refused to co-operate.

'All done?'

He pushed the thought aside as Holly leaned over
to open the door for him. Tossing his case into the
back next to her bulging rucksack, he slid behind the
wheel. 'Yep. It was a nasty burn but it should heal
all right.'

'So Helen doesn't need to go to hospital, then?'
Holly asked, settling back in the seat as he started
the engine.

'No. There was only superficial damage to the der-
mis.' He turned the car and headed back towards
town. 'So, back to you—David has no idea that
you're coming home tonight, I take it?'

'No. I...I did think about phoning him from
London...'

'But?' he prompted as she tailed off. He frowned
as he saw the uncertainty on her face. 'Come on,
Holly, what is it? Why didn't you phone your father
to let him know you were on your way home?'

'Because I wasn't sure how he'd feel about me

turning up again like this,' she admitted in a choked voice. Sam saw her eyes fill with tears before she quickly turned away. 'Maybe he won't want me back after…after the way I upped and left when Mum died.'

'Are you crazy?' He reached over and wiped a glistening teardrop from her lashes with the tip of his finger. 'David will be overjoyed that you're home at last.'

'Think so?' She tried to smile but it was a poor effort. Sam sighed as he drew the car into the side of the road. He turned her to face him, his heart aching as he saw the need for reassurance in her tear-drenched eyes.

'I know so, you idiot!' He brushed a few more tears off her cheeks, feeling his fingertips tingle as they slid across the velvety softness of her skin. He couldn't resist letting them follow the delicate contours of her cheek-bones even though he knew it was a dangerous indulgence. Touching her like this, it unleashed a host of powerful emotions inside him, most of which he barely understood.

He cleared his throat but he could hear the husky note his voice held even if she couldn't. 'Having you home again, it will be the icing on the cake so far as David is concerned.'

'What do you mean?' The puzzlement in her voice was like a dash of cold water. Sam let his hands drop, inwardly cursing the slip he'd made. Holly knew nothing about what had happened recently and it really wasn't his place to tell her. However, it was less a need to remain detached which kept him silent now than a fear that it would hurt her to hear the news.

Like it or not—which he didn't—he knew that he couldn't bear to see her upset again.

'Nothing,' he hedged, putting the car into gear and setting off again. 'All I'm trying to say is that David will be thrilled to have you home again. And you can take that as gospel.'

'I hope so.' There was a lingering uncertainty in the look she gave him but he kept his attention on the road, afraid that she'd guess that he wasn't telling her the whole truth. It didn't come easily to him to be evasive and he felt less than happy about it, but he didn't have a choice.

It was a relief when her attention was suddenly distracted as they crested the hill and she caught her first sight of Yewdale in the valley below. The night was so clear that it was possible to pick out individual houses even from that distance, an almost full moon bathing the scene in a silvery light which gave it a breathtaking beauty.

'I can't tell you how many times I've dreamt of this…' There was wonderment in her voice as she drank in the sight. She reached for his hand, clinging to it as though she needed something to hold onto to prove she wasn't dreaming.

Sam's fingers closed around hers as he felt a lump come to his throat. Her joy at seeing the town touched him all the more because he'd never felt that way about any place himself.

She turned to him, her eyes shining with pleasure, but beneath the joy there was still that same need for reassurance. 'It is going to be all right, isn't it, Sam?'

'Yes.' He had to clear his throat before he could continue. He couldn't explain it, but he knew that somehow he had to convince her. 'I promise you that everything is going to be just fine from now on, Holly.'

She stared at him for a moment longer then suddenly laughed. 'Well, that's one promise I shall keep you to, Dr O'Neill!'

She settled back in the seat as the car started down the hill. He was glad that she seemed content to sit in silence because for the life of him he couldn't have carried on a conversation at that moment.

He gripped the steering-wheel so hard that his knuckles turned white from the pressure. There was a sick feeling in the pit of his stomach, a sense of bewilderment spreading through his whole body.

What on earth had possessed him to say such a thing?

He wasn't responsible for Holly Ross's future happiness. He didn't want to be responsible for it! No ties, no commitments and *definitely* no promises he couldn't keep. Those were the rules he lived by and they had served him well up to now. So why hadn't he stuck to them?

He glanced sideways and felt his heart lurch in sudden panic. What was it about Holly that made him want to tear up the rule book—and throw it away?

CHAPTER TWO

THE town was in darkness when they drove along the high street a short time later. It was almost two a.m. and Yewdale's inhabitants were safely tucked up in their beds. Sam slowed as they came to the lane where Holly lived. Now that they were here he was having second thoughts. How could he let her go into the house without giving her some inkling of the situation she would meet there?

'I don't know if this is a good idea,' he began as he brought the car to a stop. He turned to look at her, noticing immediately the exhaustion on her face. It made it all the more difficult to decide what to do. Was she in a fit state to handle the news?

'What do you mean?' she queried with a frown.

'Oh, just that do you think it's a good idea to go waking the whole house up at this time of the night or, rather, morning?' Once again he found himself hedging rather than coming out and saying what needed to be said. He sighed, wondering why he was having such difficulty dealing with this. Holly was going to find out sooner or later what had happened, yet he couldn't get past the thought that she might be upset when she heard about her father and Laura.

She grimaced as she glanced at her watch. 'Oh! I see what you mean. I hadn't realised it was so late.' She looked along the deserted street and sighed. 'So, what do you suggest I should do, Sam?'

22

'That you come home with me and spend the night at my place,' he offered immediately, telling himself that he didn't have a choice. It wasn't that he saw her as his responsibility, for heaven's sake. It was what he would have done for anyone in such circumstances.

Pleased by such a rational explanation, he gave her a quick grin. 'I can't promise you five-star luxury but at least it'll be somewhere to sleep, and you're more than welcome to stay.'

'Thanks. It's good of you to go to all this trouble. As you say, it seems a shame to go waking everyone up at this unearthly hour.' She gave a strained laugh. 'I don't want to get off on the wrong foot, do I?'

'I keep telling you that David will be thrilled to have you home again,' Sam said, but it was obvious that she wasn't convinced. He didn't say anything more as he sped back through the town to the tiny cottage he'd been renting for the past year. It was one of a row of similar cottages, all built of grey stone and sturdy enough to withstand the changeable weather in that part of the world. It suited his needs and he'd be sorry to leave when the time came.

He drew up and switched off the engine as he glanced at the girl beside him. She looked as though she was ready to fall asleep at any second, he realised, overcome by tenderness as he noticed her drooping eyelids. Unconsciously his tone softened, 'Come on, sleepyhead, you look all in. Do you need your bag?'

'No, it's fine. Just leave it here.' She smiled tiredly. 'The only thing I need at this moment is a bed and twelve hours' sleep.'

'Well, that's easily arranged—although if we don't get you inside pretty soon then I think the bed will be surplus to requirements. Another couple of minutes and you'll be asleep in that seat,' he replied with a teasing laugh as he opened the car door. Holly got out of the car and came to join him, yawning widely as he unlocked the front door.

'I'll just switch a light on,' he informed her as he stepped inside the tiny hall. He glanced around as she followed him. 'Careful, the carpet's a bit worn by the door.'

The warning must have come a shade too late because there was a gasp and the next moment she went flying across the hall. It was pure instinct which had Sam leaping forward. He caught her before she fell, holding her tightly against him.

'Are you OK?' he asked in concern, reaching over to switch on the light so that he could see her properly.

'I think so.' Holly gave a shaky laugh. 'Talk about making a grand entrance!'

He laughed at the wry comment, feeling his pulse leap as he suddenly realised the intimacy of their position—how her slender body was resting against his from breast to thigh. She was only a couple of inches shorter than he was and in the lamplight her face had an ethereal beauty as she looked at him with those sleepy green eyes.

He carefully set her from him, his heart thundering as though he'd just run a race. 'How about a cup of tea before you go to bed?' Sam suggested in a voice that sounded unlike his own. It was difficult to pretend that everything was normal but he forced himself to try, afraid that she'd guess something was wrong. Would she be as shocked as he was by the need he'd felt just now to kiss her? He had no intention of finding out!

'No. I...I think I'll go straight up to bed if you don't mind.'

The quaver in her voice made him wonder if she'd somehow latched onto his thoughts. Sam could feel heat seeping through his whole body at the idea. He was acting like a first-class idiot and it wasn't pleasant to admit it. He liked women and they liked him so that he'd had his fair share of relationships over the years, but he felt as gauche as a teenager on a first date right then.

'Of course not. I'll show you which room you can use,' he said quickly, clamping down on such ludicrous ideas. Maybe Holly wasn't the only one who was tired around here, he thought wryly as he led the way up the narrow staircase.

'I'm afraid the spare room is only tiny but it should do just for tonight,' he said, stepping aside so that she could see inside the bedroom. He rented the cottage fully furnished so had done little to the room apart from hang a few pictures on the walls. However, the colourful patchwork quilt on the single bed and brightly woven cushion on the straight-backed chair gave the room a cosy charm.

'It's lovely, really. And I can't tell you how grateful I am, Sam—not just for letting me stay but for everything you've done tonight.' Holly's eyes were a softly luminous green as she turned to him. 'I know I was awfully rude earlier on when you offered to drive me home. My only excuse is that I've grown used to having to fend for myself this past year. I find it, well, difficult to accept help, I suppose.'

'Don't worry about it. I shan't.' Sam glanced over his shoulder, concentrating on practicalities rather than the urge to find out more about what had happened to her this past year. He might not like the idea, but he sensed that it would be only too easy to become involved in her life.

'The bathroom's straight across the landing, although ''bathroom'' is rather a misnomer as there's no bath,' he said lightly instead. 'There is a shower, though, plus all the usual amenities, and there should be plenty of hot water so help yourself.'

'I know this sounds terrible but I'm just too tired to bother about cleanliness tonight.' She stifled another yawn. 'I think I'll go straight to bed, if you don't mind.'

'Of course not.' He hesitated, oddly reluctant to leave it at that, but what else was there to say? 'Well, goodnight, then. I'll see you in the morning I expect.'

'Night, Sam.' She stepped inside the bedroom and closed the door, but for several seconds he stayed where he was. He took a deep breath but it did little to dispel the tension that was knotting his stomach once again. It was only as he heard the church clock striking the quarter-hour that he roused himself to go to his own room and got ready for bed for the second time that night.

Punching the pillow into shape, he closed his eyes and tried to relax. It had been a long day, made even longer by everything that had happened that night. He was bone tired yet it was a long time before he finally dropped off to sleep. And when he did his dreams were filled with visions of a girl with honey-brown hair and huge green eyes…

Holly Ross had come home to Yewdale and into his life—whether he liked it or not!

Sam was up before eight the next morning, although he wasn't due to work as it was Saturday and it wasn't his turn to take surgery that morning. There had been no more calls during the night so he couldn't blame them for the fact that he felt so tired.

He made himself a cup of coffee, trying not to think about the dreams which had kept him tossing and turning, but it was impossible to get them out of his head even now. He sighed as he stared out of the kitchen window. He couldn't recall ever feeling this mixed up before yet what was it about Holly which made him feel this way? Was it that air of vulnerability which touched a chord inside him? He wasn't sure but he was honest enough to admit that never before had he felt so aware of another person's feelings as he was of hers.

The doorbell rang suddenly and he frowned as he set the cup on the table and went to answer it. Who on earth could it be at this time of the morning?

'Right, are you ready, then?' Abbie Fraser, the local district nurse and his closest friend, swept into the hall as he opened the door.

'Ready?' he said blankly.

'It's Saturday morning and you're coming with me to look at that car I'm thinking of buying—remember?' Abbie sighed as she saw his expression change. 'You'd forgotten all about it, hadn't you, Sam?'

'No, of course not...' he began, then grimaced. 'Well, it might just have slipped my mind.'

'Slipped your mind, indeed.' Abbie folded her arms and glared at him. 'It was *you* who insisted on coming in the first place. What was it you said about me getting ripped off because I know nothing about cars?'

'I know, I know!' Sam held up his hands in defeat. 'Guilty as charged, your honour. And I meant every word. Your idea of choosing a car is to pick out a nice colour!'

'So what's wrong with that?' she retorted tartly, heading for the kitchen and plugging in the kettle with all the easy familiarity of a close friend.

'Nothing. But in a job like yours it would seem a *tad* more sensible to make sure that the engine isn't going to pack up the minute you try driving up one of these hills,' he replied dryly, taking a cup from the cupboard and handing it to her.

'And you can guarantee that won't happen, can you, O'Neill?' She spooned coffee into the cup, grinning at him. 'Not only Yewdale's most dashing doctor but an ace mechanic to boot! It's just a pity that you'll be the other side of the world in a few weeks' time or I'd have you put that in writing.'

Sam laughed. Since he'd come to Yewdale, he and Abbie had become firm friends and he enjoyed their verbal sparring matches. 'And have me sign it in blood, I expect.'

'Of course.' She sighed theatrically as she sipped her coffee. 'Typical of a man, though, that he leads you into a situation then makes sure he isn't around if things go wrong!'

'If you'd prefer someone else to have a look at the car…' he began, oddly stung by the comment.

'Don't be daft! I was just kidding.' Abbie frowned as she put the cup down and regarded him thoughtfully. 'It isn't like you to be so touchy, Sam. Is something wrong?'

'No, of course not.' He turned away, shuddering as he took a swallow of his own coffee and found that it had gone cold. He emptied it down the sink and set about making another, aware that Abbie was watching him intently. 'What?' he said shortly, glancing at her.

'Nothing.' She shrugged. 'If you say there's nothing wrong then I have to believe you, don't I?'

He sighed, realising that he had little option but to explain although he wasn't sure quite what he was going to say. How could he explain to Abbie why he felt so edgy when he barely understood it himself? 'Something happened last night which I'm not sure how to deal with,' he began.

'Really? Doesn't sound like the ever-confident Dr O'Neill to me,' she teased. 'Come on, tell Auntie Abbie all about it—' She broke off as the sound of the shower carried clearly down to where they both stood. 'Aha, I think I'm starting to get the picture. No wonder you forgot all about coming with me this morning.'

'It isn't what you think, Abbie,' he said quickly. He heard the shower stop then the bathroom door open, and felt his pulse leap. He turned away to fill the kettle, shocked by his response. The thought of Holly moving about upstairs as she got dressed made his heartbeat quicken and his blood race a little faster than was normal—or, indeed, comfortable!

'Isn't it? Look, Sam, this is me you're talking to. You don't have to explain. If you've had someone staying overnight that's your business.' Abbie put her cup down and headed for the door. 'I'll get out of your way. Never mind about the car. We can always make it another day—'

'It's Holly.' Sam swung round. His face was set as he stared at the ceiling. 'That's who's upstairs.'

'Holly? You mean David's daughter?' Abbie sounded stunned by the news and Sam laughed hollowly.

'Uh-huh. Got it in one.'

'But…but I thought she was in Brazil or some place like that,' she said, obviously having trouble taking in what he was saying.

'So did I until I nearly ran her over last night!' His tone was grim as he recounted what had happened. 'She came up from London by coach and had the driver drop her off at the motorway services. She was walking home from there when I came across her just after midnight.'

'Walking?' Abbie echoed. 'But it's miles from the motorway to Yewdale.'

'Don't I know it! Anything could have happened to her at that time of the night,' he agreed shortly.

'Too right.' She cast him a puzzled look. 'But why bring her back here? Why didn't you take her home, Sam? I don't understand.'

He sighed as the kettle came to the boil. He switched it off, speaking over his shoulder as he spooned coffee granules into a cup. 'Because I dis-

covered that she had no idea about David and
Laura—'

He broke off, suddenly conscious of the silence.
He glanced round and felt his heart contract as he
saw Holly standing in the doorway. She was wearing
the robe he always left behind the bathroom door,
the thick white towelling tightly belted around her
slim waist. Her hair was dripping wet, its honey-
brown colour darkened by moisture so that it made
a stark contrast to the underlying pallor of her skin.

Sam put the teaspoon down with a clatter that
sounded unnaturally loud. 'Good morning, Holly. I
hope we didn't wake you—'

'What did you mean about my father? And who
is this Laura? Tell me what's going on, Sam. I want
to know!'

There was a rising note of hysteria in her voice
that snapped him into action. He crossed the room in
a couple of strides and steered her towards a chair.
Without being asked, Abbie made a cup of coffee
and brought it back to the table.

'Do you want me to stay?' she asked quietly,
glancing in concern at the younger woman.

'No, it's OK, I'll handle this. Thanks, Abbie,' Sam
replied, his eyes never leaving Holly's face. Shock
had stolen every vestige of colour from her skin so
that her eyes appeared even more brilliant. His hands
were resting on her shoulders so that he could feel
the shudder that kept working its way through her
body in waves. He wondered if she was going to
faint, but even as the thought crossed his mind she
drew away from him and sat stiffly erect in the chair.

'I'll leave you to it, then. You know where I am

if you need me.' Abbie gave him a last worried smile before she left. Sam sat down at the table as the front door closed and took Holly's cold hands in his, but she snatched them away again.

'I had the feeling something was wrong last night…' She took another deep breath, before continuing in a harsh little monotone which cut him to the quick. 'Tell me what's happened, Sam. I think it's way past time you did that, don't you?'

'It's nothing dreadful for starters. I'm sure that once you get used to the idea you'll be as delighted as we all are,' he said flatly. It stung to know that she blamed him for not telling her the news sooner when all he'd wanted had been to make things easier for her. 'Your father has remarried. Her name is Laura Mackenzie and she's a paediatric consultant at the hospital.'

'Married? I don't believe you! It's some sort of…of silly joke.' She went to get up but he caught hold of her hands and stopped her. She glared at him with stormy green eyes. 'Let me go!'

'It isn't a joke, Holly. It's the truth. Laura bought the house next door to yours and that's how David met her.' He could feel the tension oozing from her and deliberately kept his tone level even though it was an effort to do so. It was just as he'd feared, and he hated to see her upset like this. He had no choice now but to tell her the whole story.

Without being aware of it, his hands moved to her wrists while he lightly caressed her skin. 'It was obvious to everyone that they were crazy about one another almost from the first moment they met. It wasn't for me to say, but I sensed that your father had some difficulty accepting how he felt in the beginning.'

'Because of Mum, you mean?' She laughed discordantly. 'Well, obviously it didn't take him long to get over that. He managed to forget about *her* quickly enough, didn't he?'

Sam's hands stilled. 'I don't think anyone has the right to say things like that, *especially* not you, Holly.'

She had the grace to blush at the rebuke. She stared down at the cooling cup of coffee in front of her. 'I'm sorry. You're right, of course, Sam. I...I know how much Dad loved Mum, and it was a horrible thing to say. It's just such a shock. I can't seem to take it in that he's met someone else.'

'I know it must be difficult for you. But once you meet Laura and see how happy she and David are, you'll understand, I'm sure.' He let go of her hands and tilted her chin so that she was forced to look at him. 'Just try to be open-minded about the situation, will you?'

'I'll try. I suppose I'll have to.' She took a deep breath then abruptly stood up. 'I think it would be better if I called Dad rather than just turned up on the doorstep. Do you mind if I use your phone, Sam?'

'Of course not.' He picked up the cups and carried them to the sink. He glanced round as he sensed that she was still in the room.

'I suppose you were worried about me upsetting Dad last night, weren't you, Sam? That's why you brought me back here so that I wouldn't go barging in and say the wrong thing.'

There was such need in her voice that he couldn't ignore it, despite the fact that he knew he was getting into treacherous waters, but he couldn't bring himself to lie to her. 'Partly. But the main reason I brought you back here was because I knew what a shock this would be for you.'

He looked down at the cup, focusing on the swirling pattern of leaves. Maroons were going off inside his head, warning him that he was now in serious danger, but it was impossible to turn back at this point. Sink or swim, he had to go on!

He looked up and his eyes reflected all the turmoil he felt. 'I couldn't bear the thought that *you* might be upset, if you want the truth, Holly.'

'I see.' She tried to smile but he could see that what he'd said had touched her deeply. 'Then all I can say is thank you, Sam. I…I appreciate that.'

'Don't mention it.' He laughed, deliberately trying to lighten the mood. 'I'll chalk it up on the slate along with all my other good deeds!'

Holly smiled but she didn't say anything more as she went out into the hall to make the phone call. Sam ran water into the bowl and set about washing the dishes, not wanting to hear what she was saying. He'd done his bit so it was up to her to sort things out now…

It was only as he realised that he had washed the same cup three times that he was forced to admit that it wasn't that simple. Whether he liked it or not, he was already more involved than he wanted to be!

CHAPTER THREE

SAM was glad when the weekend was over and Monday morning arrived. At least with work to concentrate on he'd have less time to think about Holly and how she was coping.

He hadn't heard a word from her since she'd left the cottage on Saturday morning. She'd refused his offer to drive her home and he hadn't pursued it. He'd sensed that she needed some time by herself to adapt to the idea of the changes she'd meet there.

That it seemed wiser to draw back from the situation himself was also a major consideration. He couldn't afford to get involved at this stage. In just over a month's time he'd be leaving England, but it was harder than he could have imagined to remain dispassionate.

He arrived at the surgery just after eight on Monday morning to find Elizabeth already bustling about in the office. 'You're early, Liz,' he commented as he closed the door.

'We've got a bit of a problem, I'm afraid.' Elizabeth sighed as she opened the diary and checked the list of appointments scheduled for that morning. 'I had a call from Eileen yesterday afternoon. Evidently her sister's been taken ill and she wanted to go up to Edinburgh to see her.'

'I see,' Sam replied thoughtfully. Eileen Pierce was the practice's receptionist. She had worked at the surgery for years and what she didn't know about running the place wasn't worth mentioning. 'You said that it was all right if she took some time off, I assume?'

'Of course. But it does leave us in a bit of mess. Usually we get Penny Watson in to cover when Eileen goes on holiday, but as luck would have it she and her family are away at the moment.' Elizabeth frowned as she glanced at the row of filing cabinets. 'I can't think of anyone who could give us a hand until Eileen gets back, can you?'

Sam shook his head. 'Not really. Have you had a word with David to see if he can come up with any suggestions?'

'Not yet. I decided not to bother him with it yesterday.' Elizabeth began getting record cards out of the drawers. 'Abbie popped round to see me on Saturday with some rather unexpected news. It seems that Holly has come home at long last. David must be thrilled, of course, so I decided that it wouldn't be fair to interrupt the family reunion—' She broke off with a laugh. 'Now there's an idea! Why didn't I think of it before?'

'What do you mean?' Sam queried, only half listening. Obviously Abbie hadn't mentioned his part in Holly's homecoming and he was glad. It was better all round if he steered clear of this situation. Holly Ross had had a decidedly strange effect on him, although he still hadn't managed to work out why.

'That Holly might be willing to help out in here,' Elizabeth explained, obviously delighted by the idea. 'I'll give David a ring and see what he thinks before

I ask her. But it seems like the ideal solution, wouldn't you agree?'

She didn't wait for an answer and picked up the phone. Sam left her to make the call, wondering why he felt less than enthusiastic about the idea. Obviously they needed help until Eileen got back but the thought that Holly might soon be working here on a daily basis was deeply unsettling.

He went to his room and got ready for his patients, telling himself that he was acting like an idiot by worrying about it. What difference would it make after all? However, he knew deep down that having Holly around all the time wasn't going to be easy to deal with. There was something about her which sparked a response in him, no matter how much he might not want it to happen...

There was the usual mix of patients to see that morning. It was the height of the tourist season and a couple of the people he saw were staying in Yewdale on holiday. It never failed to amaze him how normally sensible folk cast caution to the wind when they went away, often with disastrous consequences.

Tom Roughley was one of those. A heavy-set man in his fifties with a booming voice, he hobbled into the surgery, leaning heavily on his wife Mavis's shoulder. 'Young lady out there told me to give you this, Doctor.'

Tom handed the temporary residency form across the desk and Sam took it with a smile. He glanced at the details, quickly noting that Tom Roughley was from Oxfordshire. The form was neatly filled in but the writing was unfamiliar, and he realised that

Elizabeth's phone call must have garnered positive results. Holly must have agreed to lend a hand in their current crisis.

'Please sit down, Mr Roughley. I'm Doctor O'Neill, by the way.' Sam concentrated on his patient, cutting short any other thoughts. 'Now would you like to tell me what's happened?'

'Had a bit of an accident, water-skiing.' Tom Roughley eased himself down onto a chair with his wife's help. He grimaced as he tried to straighten his left leg. 'Seem to have done something to my knee.'

'I see.' Sam hid his surprise as he got up and went around the desk. Tom Roughley didn't look like someone who participated in such a demanding sport but, then, it was often hard to judge from appearances. 'Do you do a lot of water-skiing, Mr Roughley?'

Tom coughed, looking a shade embarrassed. 'Not really, Dr O'Neill. To tell the truth, this is the first time I've tried my hand at it.'

'And the last!' Mavis Roughley put in tartly. 'Didn't I warn you it was utter madness for a man of your age to attempt such a thing, Tom?'

'Yes, yes. Doctor doesn't want his time wasted by listening to you going on about it, Mavis,' Tom blustered, cutting short his wife's recriminations.

'Can you straighten your leg any more than that, or is that as far as it will go?' Sam asked quickly before the situation could deteriorate into an argument.

'That's it, I'm afraid.' Tom Roughley sighed. 'I tried putting an ice pack on it last night to see if that would take the swelling down, but it doesn't seem to have done much good. I still can't straighten it out.'

'Looks to me as though you could have a fragment of cartilage caught in the joint. That usually causes the knee to lock in position.' Sam stood up. 'I'd just like to examine you, Mr Roughley, so if you could slip your trousers off then I can see just how much damage has been done.'

It was quite a struggle, getting Tom Roughley undressed and onto the examination couch. His left knee was extremely swollen where fluid had gathered around the joint and even the slightest movement caused him a great deal of pain. Sam gently examined the knee and sighed as he realised that his initial diagnosis had probably been correct.

'Well, you'll need it X-rayed, Mr Roughley, but it looks to me as though the cartilage is damaged. It's easily done if the knee is twisted sharply, as probably happened in this case. I'm afraid you're going to have to go to hospital before we have a better idea of the extent of the problem.'

'There! I told you, Tom. Didn't I say that you'd end up in hospital if you persisted in trying to act like a twenty-year-old?' Mavis sounded delighted that her prediction had come true. Sam quickly stepped in to prevent another round in what was obviously an ongoing battle between husband and wife.

'I'll get onto the hospital and warn them that you're coming so that you won't have to wait too long to be seen. Have you any transport to get there, by the way?'

'Well, we've got our car but obviously I can't drive with my knee in this state.' Tom Roughley sighed. 'And Mavis doesn't drive so what do you suggest, Dr O'Neill? Are there any taxis in the town?'

'I'm afraid not. There isn't much call for them, you see.' Sam frowned as he tried to think of a solution. This was in no way an emergency so it was out of the question to call an ambulance, but there had to be a way to get Tom Roughley the twenty-odd miles to hospital.

'I could have a word with Jim Patterson at the local garage and see if he'll take you. He has a couple of cars he uses for weddings and funerals. He also drives the minibus that takes the local children to the high school each day during term time.'

'If you wouldn't mind, Doctor.' Tom gave a booming laugh. 'But ask him to leave the hearse at home, will you? Despite what Mavis keeps telling me, I'm hoping it will be a few years yet before I need to travel in one of those!'

Sam laughed as he picked up the phone. 'I'll do that.'

The waiting room was empty when he left his room after his last patient had gone. Obviously Jim Patterson had collected the Roughleys and they should be on their way to hospital by now. He hoped that they managed to keep a rein on their squabbling but Jim could be in for a hectic couple of hours from what he'd seen.

There was no sign of his colleagues so Sam assumed that the others had finished before him and gone their separate ways. There were clinics scheduled for most afternoons throughout the week, plus paperwork to catch up on, so free time was at a premium. Most of the time it was hard to snatch half an hour during the day for a break.

It was his turn to cover any house calls that day so he made his way to the office to collect the messages which had been phoned in. He had the morning's record cards in his hands and was glancing through them to check that he hadn't forgotten anything as he walked through the door. He didn't see the girl who was coming in the opposite direction.

'Oh!' Holly's gasp of dismay was echoed by his own as they collided. His cards and the tray of papers she was carrying went flying in all directions.

'Sorry!' Sam exclaimed as he looked at the mess of papers scattered all over the floor. 'I wasn't looking where I was going, I'm afraid.'

'Not to worry.' There was a husky note in her voice which he could only attribute to the shock she'd had. He gave her an apologetic smile and saw a touch of colour bloom in her cheeks before she quickly bent and began gathering the papers together.

'Here, let me help you with that,' he offered immediately, stooping down just as she started to straighten up. They bumped heads with some force and he groaned as a burst of brilliant coloured stars erupted before his eyes.

'Sorry again! Are you OK?' he asked, offering her a hand as she staggered dazedly to her feet.

'I think so…' She grimaced, probing the tender spot on her forehead where their heads had connected. 'Ouch, that hurts!'

'Let me see.' He led her out of the office and turned her face up to the overhead light. 'Oh, dear, looks as though you're going to have quite a bruise there.'

'So are you!' she retorted, staring pointedly at the reddening lump in the center of his forehead. 'We're going to look like matching book-ends!'

Sam laughed at the tart comment. 'We'll have to think up a good story to tell everyone, then.'

'You mean something a little less prosaic than we banged heads, picking up some papers?' Her grin was wicked. 'Hmm, so what do you suggest, Sam? It has to be something *really* interesting, though.'

'How about an encounter with an alien life force? We could claim that we've been subjected to an attempt to brainwash us,' he suggested, trying to keep a straight face.

'Not bad. But do you really think people will go for the idea of Yewdale being invaded by little green men?' She hooted with laughter as he shrugged comically. 'No, neither do I somehow.'

She looked up at him with dancing green eyes, her lips still parted in a smile. Sam wasn't sure what caused the sudden switch in moods yet he knew to the very second when amusement turned to something else. His heart started to knock against his ribs when he saw her eyes darken as laughter was replaced by sudden awareness, and wondered if she could hear the noise it made. It sounded so loud to him that he couldn't believe that she couldn't.

He took a slow breath, fighting to keep his tone level, but it was a waste of effort. How could he speak calmly, rationally, *dispassionately*, when his heart was turning somersaults at such an alarming rate?

'I'll have to try harder to come up with a better story, then, won't I?' he said huskily, dazzled by the rapid play of emotions that crossed her face. Was Holly finding it as difficult as he was to act normally? he wondered, then refused to work out the answer because he was afraid of what it would be.

'Yes.' She took a quick breath which made her breasts swell against the soft cotton of her pale blue dress. Sam almost groaned out loud. Did she have any idea how he was feeling at that moment? He hoped not! It wasn't easy to admit that he felt more keyed up, having this crazy conversation with her, than he'd felt at many a more intimate moment!

'You…you'll have to work on it, Sam,' she said with a laugh which was meant to be light but which didn't quite come off. She quickly turned away, hurrying into the office to fetch a small pile of message slips. 'Dad said that you were on call this afternoon so these should keep you busy.'

'Thanks.' He took the bundle from her, taking care not to let their fingers brush. His emotions were tinder dry so that it would need only the smallest spark to set them alight. He had an overwhelming urge to pull her into his arms and kiss her until they were both senseless…

'Right, I'll be off, then.' He swung round and headed for the door before instinct got the better of self-discipline. It wasn't that he'd denied himself female company—far from it—but it had always been on his terms. He'd had no trouble sticking to his rules and had always been honest about his intentions so that any relationships had ended in friendship, not tears. The last thing he'd ever wanted had been to hurt anyone.

Yet he knew in his heart that he could hurt Holly if he wasn't careful and the thought scared him rigid. He would never forgive himself if he caused her any pain.

'I'll see you later, I expect, Sam.'

There was a wistfulness in her voice which made him pause despite the fact he knew it was a mistake. He glanced round, feeling his heart thunder as he looked at her. The blue dress with its softly flowing skirt made the most of her slender figure and willowy height. She had caught her hair back from her face with two thin gold slides and the style emphasised the purity of her features.

She looked so young and lovely that he would have needed a heart of stone to remain immune. But somehow, some way, he had to get to grips with the way she made him feel otherwise it might not be only Holly who got hurt.

'I expect so,' he replied, deliberately offhand. 'We're all grateful that you agreed to help out. It will save us a lot of extra work.'

'Think nothing of it.' She drew herself up as she caught the note of detachment in his voice, which had cost him such a lot of effort. 'After all, I can't sit round all day, doing nothing. I may as well be here as anywhere else.'

She gave him a dismissive smile before she went back into the office. Sam wrenched the door open and just managed to stop himself from slamming it behind him. He'd wanted to convince her that her working here meant nothing to him, and he'd succeeded. What a pity that it didn't make him feel any better.

He got into his car and drove out of the surgery gates without looking back. It was good practice for when he left in a few weeks' time. But when he'd made his plans he hadn't taken into account that he might be sorry to leave behind some aspects of the job. Leaving Yewdale might turn out to be more difficult than he'd imagined it would be.

The rest of the day passed quickly enough. Sam had little time to brood on the events of the morning as he dealt with the home visits then followed them up with evening surgery. It was well after six when he was finally finished for the day, and he gave a wary sigh of relief as he prepared to go home. He was just making his way down the corridor when David popped his head round his door and stopped him.

'I was hoping to catch you, Sam. I just wanted to say thanks for helping Holly on Friday. I appreciate it.'

Sam shrugged. 'I didn't do anything more than anyone else would have done.'

'Well, I don't know about that...' David grimaced as he glanced along the corridor. There were still a few patients about although evening surgery was nearly at an end. 'Look, I don't want to delay you but have you got a minute?'

'Of course.' He followed David into his room, wondering what this was all about. He didn't have to wait long to find out.

'Holly told me about you giving her a bed for the night and why you did it. I appreciate it, Sam.'

'That's OK. I just thought it would be easier for all of you if she didn't just land on the doorstep in the middle of the night. I realised that she had no idea about you and Laura,' he added by way of explanation.

'She hadn't. I'd written to the last address I had for her but she'd moved on by then. I even tried contacting the embassy but they weren't able to track her down either.' David sighed. 'It can't be an easy situation for her to deal with, I imagine. Holly was very close to her mother.'

'How does she seem to be handling it so far?' Sam asked, unable to resist finding out.

'Pretty well on the surface. But Holly tends to hide her feelings so it isn't always easy to tell what she's thinking.' David smiled. 'Laura keeps telling me not to worry because Holly will work things out for herself.'

'And I'm sure she's right. Let's face it, if anyone can win Holly over it has to be Laura,' Sam replied sincerely. Like everyone else in Yewdale, he'd fallen under Laura's spell. Her genuine warmth drew people like a magnet and he could understand how David had fallen in love with her so quickly.

'You're right, of course. I don't know why I'm worrying about it when what I should be doing is planning a celebration. And what better time to celebrate Holly's homecoming than this very night?' David grinned. 'That's settled, then. Eight o'clock at the Fleece. The champagne is on me!'

'Oh, but I…' Sam began, but David was already hurrying out of the room. He sighed as he went out into the corridor and watched David rap on James's door to invite him to the party. The last thing he wanted was to get any more involved than he already was, but if he didn't turn up that night everyone would want to know why. The thought of having to explain his reasons for missing the party gave him hot and cold chills.

No ties, no commitments, no promises he couldn't keep… It was proving very difficult indeed to stick to those resolutions.

CHAPTER FOUR

SAM was the last to arrive at the Fleece that night
and a cheer went up as the others spotted him making
his way over to the corner they had commandeered
for the party.

'We were beginning to wonder if we should send
out a search party for you,' Abbie declared as she
scooted along the wooden bench to make room for
him.

'Nice to know you were worried about me,' he
replied lightly as he slid into the gap. A dozen times
since leaving work he'd tried to come up with an
excuse not to be there, but nothing had sounded convincing. In the end, he'd reconciled himself to the
fact that he had to show up. Although why he should
be so concerned about spending an evening in
Holly's company he had no idea!

'Of course we were worried. If you didn't turn up
then it meant one of us would have to pay for an
extra round of drinks,' Abbie retorted, holding up her
empty glass.

'I should have realised there was an ulterior mo-
tive to your concern.' Sam laughed, glancing ruefully
at the rest of the party. Elizabeth and James were
there, and David and Laura, of course. Mike and
Emily had been included in the celebration, too,
Mike glumly sipping the glass of lemonade shandy
which was all he had been allowed. Holly was tucked

into the corner, listening to something Emily was saying, and she didn't look up until Emily suddenly spotted him.

'Sam! Guess what, we had our tea here. And I had chicken nuggets and chips.'

'Lucky you. I wish I'd been invited,' he replied, smiling at the little girl's excitement. His gaze moved to Holly and he felt his heart kick into overdrive. It took a lot of effort to act casually. 'Hello, Holly.'

'Sam.' She gave him a quick smile then turned to say something to Laura but not before he'd seen the colour rise in her cheeks.

He looked away, struggling to keep his voice even as he wondered what had caused that reaction, but it wasn't the easiest thing he'd ever had to do. 'So what's it to be, folks? I believe it's my shout.'

'Take no notice of Abbie—this round's on me.' David waved to Harry Shaw, the licensee, who promptly brought over a tray of champagne glasses. Everyone laughed when the cork shot across the room as David set to work on the accompanying bottle. He filled the glasses then handed them round, even allowing Mike to take one.

Once everyone had a drink to hand, David raised his glass. 'I'd like to propose a toast—to Holly. It's good to have you home again, darling.'

Sam raised his glass when everyone else did. Instinctively, his gaze moved to Holly just as she looked his way. Their eyes met and held while the noisy hubbub of voices faded into the background.

Sam felt a frisson run through his body as though he'd come into contact with an electric current. Energy rushed into every cell and seemed to heighten his perception to an unbelievable degree. Suddenly he could smell the scent Holly wore even though she was sitting several feet away from him. He could also hear the soft sound of her breathing and feel the warmth of her skin. When she raised her glass he could actually *taste* the wine on his own tongue…

'Ugh! It's horrible!' Mike's exclamation of disgust broke the spell with an abruptness that made Sam's head spin. His hand was shaking as he raised his glass to his lips and let a little champagne run down his dry throat. He felt confused and disorientated, as though he'd stepped into bright light after being shut up in darkness for too long.

'Are you OK?' Abbie nudged him sharply in the ribs.

'Yes, of course.' He tried to smile but he didn't seem to have full control over his muscles any longer. He set the glass down and ran a hand through his hair just to assure himself that he could do it. What the hell was the matter with him? Why did he feel this way?

'Doesn't look much "of course" about it to me, O'Neill,' Abbie retorted in her usual pithy way, but the expression in her eyes showed her concern. 'You looked as though you'd seen a ghost for a moment back then. Or had some sort of vision,' she added, looking pointedly at Holly.

'Ghosts and visions? Is that what they teach you in nursing college?' Sam struggled to put just the right degree of amusement into his voice but he couldn't be sure he'd succeeded when his judgement was so impaired.

'Oh, you learn a lot in college. But you learn an

awful lot more once you get out into the big wide world. And one of the things you realise pretty quickly is that life has a nasty habit of throwing a spanner in the works when you least expect it.' Abbie didn't add anything more but, then, she didn't need to. Sam understood only too well what she meant.

He took a deep breath but it did little to ease the tension that was knotting his insides. He finished his champagne, hoping it would steady his nerves, but all it took was the husky sound of Holly's laughter to spoil the effect it had. He couldn't help looking at her even though he knew it was foolish to risk a repeat of what had happened.

She was leaning over to speak to Mike, teasing him about his dislike of the champagne. To all appearances she was intent on the conversation yet Sam knew that she was as aware of him as he was of her. Holly was simply playing the same game as he was, by feigning indifference, and it was a bitter-sweet torment to realise it.

A sudden beeping cut into the conversation. Laura sighed as she hunted through her pockets for her pager. 'I had a feeling this might happen. Excuse me, everyone, I'll just go and phone the hospital to see what's wrong.'

She went to the bar to use Harry's phone and came back a few minutes later. 'I'm afraid I'll have to go. One of the children who had a bone-marrow transplant a couple of days ago isn't at all well. I half expected something like this as we've had difficulty stabilising him.'

'Pity it had to happen tonight, though,' David said, standing up and smiling wryly at the group. 'Not that it's any surprise, of course. Last time we planned a get-together we ended up getting called out to that climbing accident, if you remember.'

'Who could forget it?' Sam replied, grimacing. 'It looked like a war zone when we got there, with injured climbers sprawled all over the place!'

Everyone laughed at the apt description. Laura slid out from behind the table and held her hand out to Emily. 'Come on, poppet. Time to go, I'm afraid.'

'Will you come back tonight, Laura?' Emily asked anxiously as she took Laura's hand. 'You said that we could go for a bike ride tomorrow 'cos you were off work this week.'

'I'm not sure if I'll make it home tonight, love. I might need to stay with the little boy who's so ill.' Laura bent down and gave Emily a quick hug. 'But I'll be back tomorrow morning and that's a promise. I'm looking forward to going for that bike ride too!'

Emily smiled, obviously delighted that the treat wasn't going to be missed. It was clear to all of them just how fond of Laura the little girl was, and that the feeling was reciprocated. Sam was pleased that everything was working out so well. David deserved some happiness after all he'd been through, although he couldn't help wondering how Holly felt about the situation.

'Right, we'll say goodnight, then.' David waved Holly back into her seat as she went to get up. 'No, you stay and enjoy yourself, darling. After all, this is *your* night.'

Within a few minutes they'd left. Mike had decided to go to his friend's house so he went as well.

Elizabeth glanced at her watch and exclaimed in surprise as she saw the time.

'We'll have to go, too! Father is ringing tonight to tell us when he's coming home.' She glanced at Holly. 'He's in Australia, visiting my sister at the moment, but we're expecting him back soon for the wedding.'

'So Dad said.' Holly laughed as she picked up her glass. 'I can't get over how much has happened while I've been away.'

Sam wondered if he was the only one to notice the hollow note in her voice. He glanced at the others but they seemed unaware that there might be anything wrong. Elizabeth and James left shortly afterwards, depleting their numbers to three.

Abbie drank the rest of her champagne and stood up, grinning as she reached for her bag. 'Well, you know the old saying about three being a crowd?'

'Don't be silly, Abbie—' Sam began.

'Honestly, there's no need—' Holly said at the same moment. They both stopped and looked at each other. Sam felt a wave of heat invade his limbs as he saw the awareness in her eyes before she quickly looked away.

Abbie laughed softly as she glanced from one to the other. 'Hmm, well, thanks anyway but there are a few things I need to do. Have fun, you two.'

She was gone before Sam could stop her, making her way quickly across the bar. He picked up his glass then put it down again when he saw that it was empty. He sighed, realising that he had to say something. 'I'm sorry about that. Take no notice of Abbie. She loves to tease.'

'I know. And it doesn't bother me, although I'd hate her to get the wrong idea,' Holly said with a strained little laugh.

'Wrong idea?' he asked before he could stop himself, and saw the colour sweep up her cheeks.

'About me being at your house on Saturday morning,' she explained huskily. 'I'm sure you explained to Abbie why I was there, didn't you, Sam?'

He shrugged. Abbie had accepted his explanation on Saturday but he had a feeling that she might not be so ready to believe it after tonight! 'Of course.'

'Good. I...I'd hate her to get the idea there was more to it than there actually was.' She took a quick breath before she looked at him. 'Dad was telling me what good friends you and Abbie are.'

He heard the question in her voice and looked down at his empty glass, his heart racing as he realised that she wanted to know about his relationship with Abbie. 'We are. Abbie and I are really good friends mainly because we aren't romantically involved and never have been,' he explained softly, struggling to contain his elation that it should matter to her.

'Oh, I see. I got the impression—' she stopped abruptly. 'Well, never mind. I just didn't want to make things awkward for you.'

If only she knew! he thought wryly. He might not be involved with Abbie, or anyone else for that matter, but Holly still managed to make the situation fraught just by being herself.

He quickly changed the subject, not wanting to dwell on how confused he'd felt ever since he'd picked her up on Friday night. 'So, how are things working out at home?'

'Oh, not too bad. Laura has gone out of her way to make me feel welcome, and it's obvious that she and Dad are crazy about one another.'

'But?' He smiled when she looked at him in surprise. 'There was a definite ''but'' tagged onto the end of that statement.'

She laughed. 'There wasn't meant to be. I'm trying my hardest to be positive and accept the status quo.'

'But it isn't easy, is it?' he said gently. He twirled his empty glass on the cardboard coaster. 'It's always difficult to accept changes. I know that only too well. I was thirteen when both my parents were killed in a motorway accident. I went into foster care afterwards and the people who looked after me did everything that could have been expected of them, but I never felt really part of their family.'

'How awful for you.' Holly reached across the table and touched his hand. 'I had no idea.'

'Why should you? You and I didn't have much chance to get to know each other before you went away.' He shrugged off the sympathy because it touched him a little too deeply. He rarely told anyone about his circumstances—even Abbie had no idea about his background—but he found himself wanting to share it with Holly because he sensed she'd understand.

'Ran away is a better way to describe it.' Holly sighed as she stared down at their joined hands. 'I'm not proud of what I did but I simply couldn't handle Mum dying like that. It made such a mockery of everything I'd believed in, made me question what I was doing. If all those doctors couldn't save Mum's life then what point was there in me carrying on with my studies?'

'And how do you feel about it now?' Sam asked, absently running his thumb over her fingers and surprised to find how calloused they were. He turned her hand over and studied it. Her fingers were long and well shaped, her palm narrow and very feminine, yet her skin was rough in places. Whatever she'd been doing this past year it had involved a lot of hard physical work, and he experienced a pang at the thought of what she'd been through.

'That Mum's death was something nobody could have prevented.' Her tone was reflective yet Sam had a feeling that this was something she hadn't discussed with anyone up till now. Suddenly he was glad that it was him with whom she was sharing her thoughts. He wanted to share things with her, he realised with sudden insight. Wanted her to tell him her hopes and fears. The realisation stunned him because never before had he felt this way about anyone.

'So, are you planning on going back to university or what?' His voice grated as the thought settled into his mind and he saw Holly look at him.

'I'm not sure. If I do go back then it has to be for the right reasons. You must understand that, surely, Sam?'

'I suppose so. To do this job you have to be totally committed otherwise it wouldn't work. And you're not certain yet if, by going back to university, you might not be simply taking the safe option. Is that it?'

'Yes.' She laughed ruefully. 'Why is it so easy to

explain things to you, Sam, when it's so hard to explain them to other people? You just seem to understand what I mean.'

'Do I?' He felt a frisson run down his spine because he knew what she meant. Hadn't he found himself telling her things he hadn't told anyone before? Yet it was this ease with which they communicated that worried him so much. He couldn't allow her to become dependent on him when he'd be leaving in a few weeks' time…

He caught himself up short as the truth hit him squarely on the chin—he couldn't allow *himself* to become dependent on her for that very same reason! There wasn't room in his life for this sort of relationship at this point.

He let go of her hand as he glanced towards the bar. He didn't dare look at her because he couldn't take the risk that he might see hurt in her eyes. 'Would you like something else to drink?' he offered in a deliberately cool tone so that she would know the conversation was at an end.

'No, thank you. I think I'd better go.' She fixed a smile to her mouth as she stood up, but he could see how strained it was. 'It's been good talking to you, Sam. Thanks.'

'I'll walk you home—' he began, feeling like the biggest heel going. He stopped when she gave a brittle little laugh.

'No, please, don't. I think it would be better if we left it at this.'

She turned and made her way across the bar. Sam stared after her retreating back. He had to physically stop himself from going after her but what would be the point in doing that? In five weeks' time he'd be on a plane to Africa and a whole new life. Holly could never be a part of the future he had planned.

'I see you've put Helen Walsh down on my list, Sam, with a note to have a word with you first?'

Sam looked up as Abbie came into his room. It was early on Tuesday morning and there was still half an hour to go before morning surgery began. Another restless night had left him feeling on edge so that it had been a relief to come into work. There was always paperwork to catch up with, but as he caught sight of the pile of letters on his desk he realised ruefully that he had achieved very little so far!

'Yes, I want you to have a word with Helen and see if you can persuade her to come into the surgery for a check-up,' he said, turning to work to keep other thoughts at bay.

'I see.' Abbie frowned as she came and perched on the edge of the desk. 'Do you think something is wrong with Helen other than the burn, then?'

'I'm not sure, to be honest. Harvey seems to think there is but when I tried asking Helen how she'd been feeling lately she clammed up.' He sighed as he tilted his chair back. 'I got the impression that she was trying to hide something, which is why I want you to have a word with her.'

'Well, I'll certainly do that. Mind you, it wouldn't surprise me if Helen is a bit run down. Frankly, I don't know how she copes—' Abbie stopped as James put his head round the door.

'Ah, so here you both are. Still nursing hangovers from last night, are you?' he teased.

'Fat chance of that!' Abbie retorted. 'I'll have you know, Dr Sinclair, that I was tucked up in bed with a good book by ten.'

'Is that a fact? I got the impression that the three of you were going to make a night of it,' James replied with a laugh. He glanced round as the phone started to ring, mercifully not giving her time to explain that she'd left soon after he had. Sam breathed a sigh of relief. Well meant though they would be, he could do without the inevitable questions.

'I'll get that,' James said quickly. 'I just wanted to remind you about the church fête on Saturday. Elizabeth and I called in to see the vicar on our way home last night to finalise arrangements for the wedding and he mentioned it. He said something about Sam presenting the first-aid badges to the Guides?'

'Oh, yes.' Abbie looked sheepish. 'I forgot to mention it, didn't I, Sam? But Mrs Delaney who runs the Guides asked me weeks ago if you'd do it. You will, won't you?'

'I suppose so. But I don't know why she's asked me,' he replied, frowning. 'Surely Liz or David would have been first choice?'

Abbie grinned as she got up. 'Oh, the girls had a vote on who they wanted to present the badges. James was a strong contender but the fact that he's engaged and spoken for went against him. So the honour fell to you, Dr O'Neill.' She sighed, pressing a hand dramatically to her heart. 'How does it feel to be the object of all that unrequited love?'

'I'll give you unrequited love, Nurse Fraser!' Sam picked up a file and made as though to throw it at her. He laughed as she made a hasty exit with James hard on her heels. He was still smiling as he got up to make a note of the fête on his weekly plan chart.

He glanced out of the window as a car door slammed and saw Holly walking across the car park. The sun was behind her, turning her hair to a golden nimbus around her head.

Sam felt his heart begin to drum. Suddenly the thought of unrequited love didn't seem funny any more. It must be painful to fall in love and not have your feelings returned, he thought.

He took a deep breath. Almost as painful as realising that you had no right to fall in love if you couldn't offer total commitment as well.

CHAPTER FIVE

SATURDAY morning dawned, bringing with it a change in the weather. The sky was heavy with rain clouds, the air cooler than it had been for weeks. When Sam went to do his shopping the main topic of conversation along the high street was whether or not the fête would be rained off that afternoon.

He went into the café after he'd finished and sat down at a table by the window, ordering coffee and a tea cake when the waitress came over. The place was even more crowded than usual and he'd got the last free table. It was the bank holiday weekend and the number of visitors had been swelled by an influx of day-trippers, although there were still a lot of local people about. There was no supermarket in the vicinity of Yewdale so most people bought what they needed at the local shops.

Sam smiled as he thought back to when he'd first arrived in the town. He'd been horrified to discover that he wouldn't be able to pop out to the supermarket at any hour of the day or night. Now he enjoyed the more leisurely pace, and had grown used to making his purchases—and the odd diagnosis—over the counter.

What a difference a year could make! he thought wryly. But he was going to have to adapt to a whole new way of life once again in the very near future...

'Do you mind if I sit here?'

He glanced up as someone stopped by his table,

feeling his heart leap as he saw Holly. He shot to his feet, almost overturning the chair in his haste. He hurriedly righted it, using the few seconds it took to get himself in hand.

'Of course not,' he replied, with what he hoped was convincing composure, but he could feel his heart tap-dancing away with a speed Fred Astaire would have envied.

'Thanks.' She sat down and gave him a quick smile. 'It's really busy in here today, isn't it? I wouldn't have disturbed you but this was the only free seat.'

Well, that put him firmly in his place. Sam fixed a smile to his own mouth, determined not to let her see how deflated he felt. 'Don't worry about it. Anyway, you're not disturbing me. I'd just stopped off for a coffee, before hauling this little lot home.'

He nodded towards the laden shopping bag tucked under the table and she laughed. 'Oh, I see. So you were wondering what you'd forgotten, were you?' She carried on when she saw his brows lift. 'You looked lost in thought when I last spotted you.'

'Did I?' He sighed as he leaned back in his chair. 'I was just thinking about how I'd adapted to living here, and how I was going to have to adapt again in a few weeks' time.'

'When you go to Africa, you mean?' Holly picked up a packet of sugar as the waitress set a cup of coffee in front of her. She ripped the top off and poured some sugar into the cup without looking at him. 'Dad told me that you fly out the first week in October. You must be excited about it, I imagine.'

'I am.' He tried to inject some of that excitement into his voice but it was difficult. He picked up a spoon and stirred his coffee, watching the frothy liquid swirling round the cup. 'It's something I've always wanted to do.'

'Then it must be wonderful to know that you're going to see your dream come true. Obviously, you won't have any last-minute change of heart.' She laughed lightly but there was a note in her voice which made a ripple run under his skin.

He took a deep breath as he struggled to ignore it. Since Tuesday when he'd seen Holly crossing the car park he'd gone out of his way to avoid being alone with her. It hadn't been difficult as the surgery had been busy and opportunities to chat hadn't been exactly thick on the ground. But he knew that he could have found the odd minute if he'd wanted to. It was the fact that he'd wanted to *so* much that had stopped him.

He couldn't afford to let his feelings override common sense. And he had to remember that now. 'Oh, there's no chance of that. Everything is arranged and I can't wait to get started,' he replied lightly.

'I see. It must be wonderful to know what you want and not have doubts about what you're doing.'

If only she knew. Doubts which had been alien to him just a week ago were suddenly sprouting faster than he cared to admit. Was he doing the right thing by turning his back on what was here? But what was here for him? It was the uncertainty which was worst because he wasn't used to being so indecisive.

'I imagine so. Anyway, that's enough about my plans. How about you? Have you decided yet what you're going to do?' he asked to change the subject.

'Not yet.' She grimaced. 'Unlike you, Sam, I find it hard to make a decision and stick to it. I keep

wavering between going back to university and finding a job.'

'Doing what?' Sam frowned.

'I don't know. Working in a shop or an office,
anything—' She broke off as there was a loud crash
from the far side of the room. Both of them turned
to see what was happening and saw the waitress hurrying over to help someone up from the floor.

'Isn't that Helen Walsh?' Holly asked, glancing at
him.

'It is. I'll just go and see if she's all right,' he
replied, quickly getting up from his seat and hurrying
across the room. 'Are you all right, Helen?' he asked,
helping the waitress sit her down on a chair.

'Yes, I'm fine.' Helen gave him a wobbly smile.
'I must have caught my foot on the table leg. Clumsy
of me, wasn't it?'

Sam smiled sympathetically. He put out a restrain-
ing hand as she went to get up. 'Just take a moment
to catch your breath. You must have given yourself
a bit of fright, I expect.'

Helen laughed, obviously determined to make
light of what had happened. 'Oh, I'll live, Dr O'Neill.
There's no need to fuss.'

Sam frowned, wondering if it was his imagination
that Helen's speech sounded rather slurred. He
glanced round as Holly came to join them and raised
his brows meaningfully. 'Helen caught her foot on
the table leg,' he explained neutrally.

'Oh, I see.' Holly's tone was as even as his had
been but he knew from the searching look she gave
the older woman that she'd understood he was concerned. 'It's easily done, isn't it, Helen? Especially
when you're loaded down with shopping like that.'

'It is,' Helen replied, obviously relieved that she wasn't going to be cross-questioned anymore. She gathered up her shopping, obviously intent on leaving as fast as she could.

'Let me help you, Helen,' Sam offered immediately, reaching for one of the plastic carriers, but she snatched it away.

'I can manage.' She must have realised how rude that had sounded because she flushed. 'Thank you, anyway, Dr O'Neill. Harvey is meeting me outside the post office so I've not got far to go.' She started to leave then paused. 'Oh, if you see Harvey, would you mind not mentioning what's happened? There's no point in him worrying when there's no need.'

She quickly made her way from the café. Sam followed Holly back to their table and sat down again, frowning as he thought about what had happened.

'You think there's something wrong with Helen, don't you, Sam?'

He sighed. 'I'm not sure. I know Harvey thinks there is. He was very concerned about her when I was called out to the farm the other night, said that she hasn't been herself lately. Did you think she sounded odd just now, as though her speech was slurred?'

'Yes. I noticed it immediately. She seemed to be having difficulty in getting the words out.'

'That's what I thought. And these accidents she keeps having all the time—it's very strange. I asked Abbie to see if she could persuade her to come into the surgery, but Helen wouldn't hear of it. Abbie said that she got quite annoyed when she tried to pursue it,' he added.

'Which isn't like Helen at all. I've known her for

years and she's always been one of the nicest people you could hope to meet.' Holly looked down at the table mat, worrying the fringed end. Sam had the impression that there was something troubling her.

'What is it?' he asked quietly.

She looked up and grimaced. 'I know this sounds an awful thing to say, but you don't think Helen was drunk, do you? There was just something about the way she was behaving...' She tailed off uncertainly.

He frowned as he thought about it. 'That could explain the slurred speech, I suppose.'

'And the number of accidents she keeps having.' She sighed. 'But Helen Walsh? No, it doesn't add up.'

'Because she's never shown any signs of drink dependency in the past, you mean?' He ran his hand through his thick black hair and sighed. 'I wish it were that simple, but many alcoholics manage to hide their behaviour for years without anyone suspecting. It's only when they reach a certain point that the problem becomes apparent.'

'How do you set about finding out if that is what's wrong with Helen?' Holly looked at him curiously. 'It wouldn't be easy even to mention it to Harvey, I don't imagine?'

'You're right. And in all truth it isn't any of our business. Until Helen asks for help our hands are tied,' he admitted sadly.

'Then we'll have to find a way round it and see if we can get to the bottom of this without her co-operation. Helen and Harvey are both too nice to have their lives ruined,' she said determinedly. She frowned as Sam laughed. 'What?'

'I get the idea that once you make up your mind

about something you aren't easily swayed,' he teased.

'You're right,' she agreed. Her eyes were an intense green as they met his. 'In that respect we have a lot in common, Sam.'

He didn't know what to say. It sounded crazy but he knew that she was telling him that she understood he'd made up his mind about them—that there wouldn't be a 'them,' in fact.

They left the coffee-shop a few minutes later and went their separate ways. Sam took a deep breath as he walked down the street, wondering why it felt as if there was a lead weight attached to his heart. There was no room in his life for a relationship at this point but it didn't stop him suddenly wishing that things could be different.

Surprisingly the rain held off and the fête went ahead as planned despite grey skies overhead. It was held in the church grounds and Sam arrived to find most of the townsfolk there along with a good many tourists. A variety of stalls had been set up, ranging from produce stalls to old-fashioned fairground games. He had a go on the hoopla stall and groaned as he succeeded in winning a goldfish in a plastic bag.

'I've no idea what I'm going to do with this!' he exclaimed, accepting the prize from a grinning Jim Patterson, who was running the stall with his fiancée, Cathy Fielding.

'Be good company for you on a cold night, Doc,' Jim said with a wink. 'And the good thing about a fish is that it can't talk your ears off, unlike most women!'

'Why, of all the cheek!' Cathy retorted, playfully

punching Jim on the arm. He gave her a hug, grinning at Sam over the top of her head.

'Of course that doesn't apply to you, my precious.'

'Mmm, I don't think,' Cathy retorted, rolling her eyes at the lavish endearment. 'How about another go, Dr O'Neill, to see if you can win a friend for Jaws here?'

'No way! One is more than enough, thank you very much,' Sam replied, hastily backing away.

'Looks as though you've hit the jackpot there all right, Dr O'Neill.'

He looked round at the sound of a familiar booming voice and saw Tom Roughley hobbling towards him with the aid of a pair of metal crutches. 'Hello, Mr Roughley. How are you doing? It doesn't look as though you're letting that knee stop you getting about.'

'Oh, take more than this to keep a good man down.' Tom came to an ungainly halt and glanced down at his heavily bandaged left knee. 'You were right about it being the cartilage, Dr O'Neill. A bit of it had got trapped in the joint. They managed to manipulate it back into place at the hospital but I wouldn't want to go through that again, I can tell you!'

'I don't wonder.' Sam grimaced. 'I believe it can be very uncomfortable. You want to be careful, though. Don't go putting too much strain on that joint or you could find yourself back at the hospital sooner than expected.'

'Oh, it'll be fine. A couple more days and it will be right as rain.' Tom brushed aside the advice. Digging into his pocket, he produced fifty pence. 'Right, let's see how well I do at this. Haven't played hoopla since I was a youngster but I doubt I've lost my touch.'

It was tricky, balancing on one leg, but Tom succeeded in putting the first hoop neatly over a peg, to his obvious delight. A second hoop swiftly joined it. He was just getting ready for the last and hopefully winning throw when his wife suddenly appeared.

'Leave you alone for five minutes and this is what you get up to, Tom Roughley. Didn't they tell you at the hospital that you had to rest that leg? You don't have the sense you were born with.'

The hoop missed its target by several inches. Sam excused himself and made a quick getaway, not wanting to be drawn into the ensuing argument. He was still smiling to himself about the Roughleys' ongoing battle when he bumped into Abbie.

'Hi, there. It's a good turnout today, isn't it?' he said lightly, glancing round at the crowd.

'It is,' Abbie replied flatly. 'The prizes are being presented at three-thirty in front of the flower tent, Sam. Can you be there about five minutes beforehand so I can run through what you need to do?'

'Of course. I didn't realise you were in charge of the prize-giving,' he said, frowning as he saw how drawn she looked.

'I wasn't meant to be. Mrs Delaney always organises it,' she explained, 'but she rang me this morning to ask if I could take over from her. She'd just heard that her son had been involved in a car accident. She and Major Delaney have driven down to London to be with him.'

'How awful for them,' Sam sympathised. 'I take it that you know him?'

'Nick? Oh, yes.' She looked away but not before

Sam had seen the look of pain that crossed her face.
'Nick and I knew one another quite well at one time,
but there's been a lot of water under the bridge since
then.'

Maybe there had, Sam thought as she hurried
away, but it hadn't washed away the memories, obviously, or the news of Nick Delaney's accident
wouldn't have hit her so hard. He wished there was
something he could do to help but he knew that
Abbie wouldn't welcome him interfering.

The afternoon passed remarkably quickly so that
before Sam could blink it was time to present the
badges to the Guides. He made a short speech, prais-
ing their efforts, then stepped down from the podium
with a sigh of relief. People were beginning to drift
away now that the main events were over so he decided it was time he went as well.

He collected the goldfish from where he'd left it
under one of the tables and set off across the field.
He spotted James and Elizabeth ahead of him and
waved, then saw Emily with Mike and a gang of his
friends. The little girl made a beeline for him as soon
as she saw what he was carrying.

'Oh, Sam, you've won a fish! Isn't he just gor-
geous?' she exclaimed, staring, entranced, at the
plastic bag in which the fish was happily swimming
around.

'Do you like him?' Sam asked, suddenly seeing a
way out of his predicament. 'Actually, I wonder if
you could do me a big favour, Emily. I need someone
to look after Jaws here, and I thought maybe you
would do it. I won't have time to take care of him
properly, with being at work, you see.'

'Really?' She clapped her hands in delight. 'Are you sure, Sam?'

'Of course,' he replied solemnly. He looked up as Mike came over. 'Hi, there. I was just asking Emily if she would look after the fish for me. Do you think your dad would mind?'

'Don't think so.' Mike shrugged. 'He's gone to town with Laura because she's on call this weekend, but I can't see that it's a problem. Why don't you check with Holly?'

Mike looked around as Danny Shepherd shouted to him, pointing at his watch. 'Holly's helping out in the tea tent so you could go over there and ask her. She said she'd be finished by four and it's almost that now. And would you mind taking Emily with you? We're all going into town to see a film and we're going to miss the bus if we don't leave now.'

'Of course not. You go ahead, Mike. Emily will be fine with me,' Sam assured the boy.

Mike hurried off while Sam headed back across the field. Emily skipped along beside him, chattering away non-stop about the fête and everything she'd done. Sam was only half listening because his mind was racing ahead to when he'd see Holly again. Suddenly he couldn't wait to be with her and the realisation stunned him because it had never happened before.

'Katie… Oh, help… Someone, please, help!'

He swung round as he heard the woman's frantic cries although it took him a moment to spot her because of the crowd. She was kneeling on the grass close to the flower tent. There was an overturned pram beside her and a small child lying on the ground, but that was all he saw before the crowd shifted and they disappeared from sight.

'Here, Emily, hold this for me.' Sam thrust the goldfish into the little girl's hands then raced across the grass. Pushing his way through the throng, he knelt down beside the mother and child and discovered that he wasn't first on the scene. Holly had got there ahead of him.

'What happened?' he asked, looking to her to explain rather than the hysterical mother.

'The child was stung by a wasp,' she replied tersely. 'I was just coming to find Mike when I heard the mother scream for help.'

'Right.' He didn't waste any time as he began to examine the little girl. She was about three years old and wheezing heavily as she tried to breathe. 'Put something under her legs to increase the blood supply to the brain—there, that bag should do.'

Holly grabbed a large shopping bag from the bottom of the pram and slipped it beneath the little girl's legs but her condition didn't improve. Each breath was increasingly laboured as her airway went into spasm.

'She must be allergic to the wasp venom,' Holly said worriedly, watching the child fighting for breath.

'Yes. She's showing all the signs of anaphylactic shock.' He looked around and spotted one of the Guides he'd just presented with a badge among the group of onlookers. 'Run to the vicarage and phone the surgery, Jessica. Tell Dr Allen that we need an injection of adrenaline immediately. And get her to phone for an ambulance as well.'

'Here, use my mobile. It will save time.' Tom

Roughley pushed through the crowd and handed him the phone.

'Thanks.' He quickly made the call, his attention never leaving the little girl so that he saw immediately when she suddenly stopped breathing. Thrusting the phone back into Tom's hand, he turned to Holly.

'Breathing's stopped. Have we got a pulse?'

She checked the carotid artery in the child's neck and shook her head. 'No. Nothing.'

'Katie! Oh, Katie!' The child's mother was almost beside herself as she realised what was happening. Sam blocked out her wails by focusing his attention on what had to be done.

'We need to give her CPR. All right?' he asked softly, looking at Holly.

'Yes.' She'd gone very pale but she didn't hesitate. 'One breath to five compressions? Is that right?'

'That's it.' He gave her a quick smile. 'I'll do the compressions, you do the breathing. But remember that she's only a young child so take it very gently.'

It was a nerve-racking experience. Because Katie was so small, they had to modify their technique, using the gentlest of breaths to puff air into her tiny body and the lightest of pressure to compress her chest. All the time, Sam was aware of how much damage could be done if they used too much force.

'I've got the adrenaline, Sam. Here.' Elizabeth arrived out of breath from the frantic dash from the surgery. Sam took the syringe and quickly administered the drug. He checked Katie's pulse, willing the adrenaline to work…

'Yes!' His cry of delight was echoed by a spontaneous burst of applause from the crowd as the little girl gasped then started to cry. Without even thinking he reached over and hugged Holly. 'We did it! We really did it!'

Tears of relief ran down her face as she hugged him back. 'I never thought.... It's just...'

'The best thing ever to know that you've saved a life,' he finished for her softly, knowing exactly how she felt.

'Yes.' Her voice was barely above a whisper as she met his eyes. 'That's it exactly, Sam.'

He took a deep breath as he let her go. Elizabeth had brought her bag with her and between them they checked the little girl over, monitoring her heartbeat and breathing. It was a relief to focus on the task because it gave him an excuse not to think about anything else. That moment of shared closeness had shaken him more than he cared to admit, especially as he sensed it had had the same effect on Holly.

Katie's mother cradled her daughter in her arms once they'd pronounced the little girl out of danger. 'I don't know how to thank you...both of you...' she began, before emotion got the better of her.

Sam patted her shoulder. 'It's OK. Katie should be fine now but you need to go to the hospital so she can be given a thorough examination. Then when you get back home you must visit your own GP and tell him what happened.'

'Could it happen again?' The young mother shuddered. 'I couldn't bear it!'

'That's why you need to speak to your own doctor. Obviously, Katie is allergic to the venom in wasp stings. That means it could happen again if she ever gets stung,' he explained gently. 'Your doctor will probably recommend that you carry a dose of adrenaline with you so that you can administer it to her if need be.'

'We haven't got a doctor. We only just moved here, you see.' The young woman wiped her eyes with the back of her hand. 'We're staying with my brother until we get sorted out.'

'Oh, so who's that?' Sam queried.

'Barry Jackson. I'm Tracey, his sister. Do you know him?'

'Yes, of course. In that case, you must come into the surgery and register with us even if it is only for a short time.' He looked round at the sound of an ambulance siren. 'Ah, here they come. We'll soon have you and Katie off to hospital.'

'Can you let Annie and Barry know what's happened, Doctor?' Tracey looked anxiously around as the ambulance made its way across the field. 'I brought their boys with me but I don't know where they've gone.'

'Don't you worry about them,' Sam advised her with the confidence of experience. He'd got to know the Jackson family soon after he'd arrived in Yewdale. Hardly a month went by when one of the five children wasn't brought into the surgery. Thankfully, it was usually for something minor, although the youngest child, Chloe, had been very ill recently after being diagnosed as suffering from leukaemia.

The three boys were real little rips, though, and always up to mischief, but they had a healthy regard for their own skins so he wasn't unduly worried about their disappearance. Neither was Elizabeth, who added her reassurances to his.

The paramedics loaded Katie and her mother into

the ambulance. Sam explained what had happened then waved them off. The crowd had started to disperse and the field was emptying fast.

'Well done, you two.' Elizabeth smiled as she looked from him to Holly. 'You make a first-rate team.'

He bent down to clear away the used hypodermic syringe, popping it into the sharps' box. Him and Holly a team? That was the one thing they could never be!

'Right, do you want me to go and tell the Jacksons what's happened?' Elizabeth asked, diplomatically ignoring the rather uncomfortable silence.

'No, I'll do it.' He stood up, carefully avoiding looking at Holly because he didn't want to see how she felt about them being paired off. 'I have to pass their house on my way home so there's no sense in you going out of your way, Liz.'

'That's fine by me. I'll get off back home, then.' Elizabeth glanced at the sky and grimaced. 'Looks like we're going to have a downpour at any moment.'

She hurried off and Holly sighed. 'Well, that's that. Thank heavens it worked out as well as it did.'

Her tone was light enough but he knew that Elizabeth's remark had touched a nerve in both of them. Luckily Emily came over just then and claimed their attention.

'Have you asked Holly if it's all right for me to mind Jaws, Sam?' she asked, with a child's eye to the priorities.

'No, not yet. Sorry.' He looked at Holly and shrugged. 'Is it OK, do you think?'

'I can't see why not—although what Peebody is going to make of having a rival for your affections,

Em, I've no idea,' Holly teased, referring to the huge, ungainly dog who was Emily's constant companion.

'Oh, he won't mind. Peebody will love him,' Emily assured them blithely.

Holly caught his eye, her rueful expression making him smile. They both laughed and the laughter helped ease any awkwardness. Most people were hurrying to get away before the rain began and it seemed the most natural thing in the world for them to leave together and walk back through the town. They had to pass the Jacksons' house and Sam knocked on the door to tell them what had happened.

'Oh, dear. As if poor Tracey hasn't got enough on her plate at the moment,' Annie Jackson said in concern. She broke off as Chloe suddenly appeared at her side. The little girl's face lit up when she saw what Emily was carrying.

'A fish! Where did you get it?'

Emily explained and Chloe's face clouded. 'I couldn't go to the fair. Dr Laura told Mummy that I might get germs.'

'It's because of her treatment, you see. With her having that bone-marrow transplant, Dr Mackenzie said that we must avoid crowded places to cut down the risk of Chloe catching anything.' Annie sighed. 'It's a real shame 'cos it's her birthday tomorrow and it would have been a treat for her. I know, maybe Emily could stay and have her tea with us, then Chloe can have a bit of a party.'

'Can I, Holly?' Emily asked immediately. 'I'll be good, promise.'

'I suppose so.' Holly smiled as the two girls ran off up the hall. 'What time shall I pick her up, Annie?'

'Oh, it doesn't matter to me. You come whenever you like, love.' Annie looked pointedly at Sam. 'It will give you two a bit of time on your own, won't it?'

What was going on around here? First Elizabeth and now Annie Jackson seemed set on making something out of nothing...

Only it wasn't nothing, was it? he realised with a sinking heart. That's where the problem lay. If he could feel about Holly as he'd felt about other women in the past then it would be a lot easier to handle the situation.

They were both a little subdued as they left the house. Sam had no idea what Holly was thinking and didn't ask. It seemed safer not to go asking questions which might elicit answers he couldn't deal with. It was a relief when the heavens opened and the rain began.

Holly bade him a quick goodbye then hurried off home. Sam made his way back to the cottage and let himself in. He went into the sitting-room and stood by the window, watching the rain slanting across the mountains.

Closing his eyes, he tried to picture where he'd be in a few weeks' time. It was something he'd done a hundred times before but today it proved impossible to imagine it.

Africa seemed an awfully long way away all of a sudden...

CHAPTER SIX

'IT LOOKS like rubella to me. When did the rash first appear?'

Sam turned to Ian Farnsworth, who ran the Outward Bound centre which was set on the banks of Yewdale Water, a couple of miles outside town. Sam had been called there first thing on Sunday morning and had been glad of the excuse to get out of the house.

He'd spent Saturday night packing, although it was really too soon to make a start on it. There were still four weeks to go before he was due to leave but he'd told himself that he needed to sort out what he was taking with him. Now the cottage looked like a tip, with boxes piled up in every corner. It was proof that he'd be leaving but it certainly hadn't helped settle his mind.

'Just after breakfast.' Ian sighed as he looked at the twelve-year-old boy. The child had a shock of bright red hair which clashed with the deep pink rash that covered him from the neck down. 'Jason complained of a headache last night. He had a bit of temperature as well, although nothing to worry about. I gave him some paracetamol and he seemed to perk up. His group was due to go swimming this morning and it was when he got into his trunks that we noticed the rash. I called you straight away.'

'I see.' Sam smiled at the glum-faced boy. 'Well, no swimming for you, Jason, I'm afraid. You're going to have to spend a few days in bed right here in the sanatorium.'

'That's not fair!' Jason was obviously upset by the news. 'I'm going to miss everything now.'

'I'm sorry, son, but there's nothing to be done about it. I'm sure Mr Farnsworth will find you some books to keep you busy.'

Jason's mutinous expression showed what he felt about that idea. Sam sighed as he followed Ian out of the room. 'I don't think I'm that young man's favourite person somehow!'

Ian laughed. 'Doesn't look like it. Mind you, I can understand how he feels. It must be rotten, knowing that all your friends are out enjoying themselves while you're stuck in bed. Jason's party only arrived yesterday so, what with the rain and everything, he hasn't had time to have a go at any of the activities yet. Let's just hope none of the others come down with it. I don't relish the idea of a san. full of bored twelve-year-olds!'

'I don't blame you, but hopefully you won't get any more cases. Most children have the MMR vaccine nowadays, which gives protection against rubella, so I doubt you'll get an outbreak.'

'I hope not. This particular group is from an inner-city youth project and they're not the easiest to work with. It's the first time most of the kids have been to the country and they tend to run wild. It's going to be a very long week even without an epidemic of German measles to contend with.'

Sam headed back home after leaving the centre. It had rained non-stop all night but the sun had come out again that morning. Now there was a hazy mist over the countryside as the moisture evaporated.

He took his time, enjoying the play of light and shadow as clouds scudded across the mountains. This part of Cumbria was particularly beautiful and on a day like this he almost wished he could stay here for ever—

He drew himself up short. He had set out his stall a long time ago and it was too late to change his mind now. He was going to Africa because it was what he wanted to do. He didn't want to look back in ten years time and regret not going.

But when he'd made those plans there had been nothing to keep him there, a small voice whispered. In ten years' time would he look back and regret not *staying*?

He sighed heavily because it was impossible to know the answer to that question. He switched on the radio, determined to put it out of his mind. He was humming along to a pop tune as he came to a bend in the road so that what happened next took him completely by surprise. He had just a second to spot the cyclist pedalling in the opposite direction and realise it was Holly before another car overtook him on the bend.

He jammed on his brakes, his heart leaping into his throat as he saw the bike lying on the ground. Pulling his car onto the grass verge, he jumped out and ran over to her.

'Are you all right?' he asked anxiously as he knelt down beside her.

'I think so.' She grimaced as she saw a trickle of blood oozing through the ragged tear in her jeans. 'I've cut my knee but it could have been a lot worse. What on earth was that idiot thinking of!'

'Heaven knows.' Sam stared along the road but

there was no sign of the car. He offered Holly his hand as she scrambled to her feet, trying not to dwell on how it made him feel to imagine her badly hurt. 'What are you doing out here at this time of the morning, anyway?'

'I was going over to the lake to do some sketching.' She bent down and retrieved her sketch pad from where it had landed in a puddle. 'Oh, look at it. It's ruined!'

'It isn't the only thing, I'm afraid. Your front wheel doesn't look too healthy either.' He righted the bike, staring grimly at the buckled wheel. It was a sharp reminder of how close to disaster she'd come.

'Damn! That's all I need.' She glared at the bike. 'What on earth am I going to do now?'

'I'll run you home,' he offered immediately, hefting the bike and carrying it over to his car. He unlocked the boot and dropped the rear seats then managed to squeeze the bike into the back.

'Are you sure you don't mind?' she asked, brushing her hair off her cheek with a grimy hand and leaving behind a smear of mud. 'I don't want to be any trouble—'

'Don't be silly.' Sam cut her off abruptly. He slammed the boot lid, struggling to contain the urge he felt to wipe that smudge off her cheek. He could just imagine how smooth and soft her skin would feel...

'Right, have we got everything? You've not dropped anything on the grass?' he asked, quickly curtailing such fantasies.

'I don't think so...' She patted her pockets then shook her head. 'No, nothing missing.'

He helped her into the passenger seat then started

the engine. It didn't take very long to reach her house and Holly seemed content to sit listening to the radio. Sam guessed that the accident had given her a scare, although she tried her best to make light of it as they drew up.

'Thanks for coming to my rescue yet again, Sam. I don't know how I would have got home otherwise.'

'Is David not back yet, then?' he asked, getting out to lift her bike from the boot and prop it against the wall.

'He popped back earlier but he didn't stop long. He just wanted to collect Emily. Laura had promised to show her where she worked.' Holly grimaced as she hobbled towards the house. 'This knee is starting to stiffen up already.'

'I'd better take a look at it,' he said immediately, holding up his hand when she started to protest. 'Doctor's orders!'

She grinned cheekily. 'Well, I can't argue with that, can I? Anyway, come in and have a coffee. I could do with a cup to steady my jangling nerves.'

He followed her into the kitchen and looked around warily. 'Where's the dog this morning? I'm usually flat on my back by now, with him licking the life out of me.'

She laughed at the wry note in his voice. 'Peebody does tend to get a little over-enthusiastic when anyone calls, doesn't he? You're safe this morning because Dad took him with them.' She pointed to the cut-glass fruit bowl on the dresser, in which the goldfish was happily swimming around, as she picked up the kettle. 'Emily wanted to take Jaws along as well but Dad drew the line at having a fish for a passenger.'

'I don't blame him.' Sam laughed at the idea. He hurriedly took the kettle out of her hand as she hobbled towards the sink. 'Let me do that. You sit down and rest that leg.'

'It's only a graze,' she protested. 'I had far worse when I was a kid. I was *always* falling over and cutting my knees. Dad says that he used up more Elastoplast on me than he's used on all his patients put together over the last twenty years!'

'Well, that's as maybe but I'd be happier if I just checked it out. So humour me, eh?'

'Well, I suppose I'll have to, seeing as you did your Sir Galahad act and came to my rescue again.' Her expression was wryly resigned as she pulled out a chair and sat down. Rolling up the leg of her jeans, she offered her knee for his inspection.

Sam plugged in the kettle then crouched down in front of her to examine the cut. 'Well, I think you'll live, but it could do with cleaning up and a dressing on it. Have you a first-aid box anywhere about?'

'In the bathroom cabinet. I'll get it—'

He pressed her back into the chair. 'You sit there. I'm sure I can find it.'

It didn't take him long to find what he needed. He went back to the kitchen and ran water into a bowl, then knelt down in front of her to clean the cut. He propped her foot on his knee, his hand lightly gripping her calf to keep her leg steady so that he felt the shiver which danced over her skin.

He looked up with a frown. 'Sorry, did that hurt?'

She shook her head so that the silky brown curls swirled around her shoulders. 'Not…not really.'

There was a husky note in her voice which sent a wave of heat through his veins. He turned his attention back to what he was doing but his hand wasn't quite steady as he squeezed a little antiseptic cream onto a clean pad of gauze.

'This might sting a bit,' he advised, without looking up.

'I'll try to be brave,' she said lightly, but he knew that she was just putting up a front. Holly was as aware of him as he was of her, and it made his heart race to know it.

He kept his attention firmly on the task as he gently attended to the graze then covered it with an adhesive dressing. 'That should do it,' he said thickly, putting her foot back on the floor.

'Thank you.' Her voice held a note that brought his eyes to her face even though he knew it was a mistake. Sam felt his heartbeat quicken until its pounding filled his whole body. He could hear it drumming in his ears so that he couldn't hear anything else except the tiny indrawn breath she took. Everything seemed to be happening in slow motion as she reached out and laid her hand lightly on his shoulder.

'Sam?'

The thundering seemed to increase as he heard the invitation that single word held. He knew he should resist it but it was impossible when every cell in his body was clamouring to respond. His hand slid up her arm to her shoulder then moved around the back of her neck.

Her hair was cool against his knuckles, the skin on her nape warm against his palm. Sam felt a spasm run from his fingertips to the soles of his feet, felt the tremor which ran through her as his hand settled into place. He knew he was holding his breath just as she was holding hers, and marvelled that they were so attuned. When he started to draw her head down towards him she moved at the very same moment so that his hand did no more than cup the back of her neck.

Their lips touched, tasted and then drew apart as though both of them needed to savour this first contact. Sam could feel the warmth of her mouth imprinted on his and knew that Holly was feeling the very same thing, that the warmth of *his* lips was imprinted on hers. It shook him.

'Holly.' Her name was little more than a whisper but he knew she'd heard it as she bent towards him once more. It was strange but they seemed to know just what to do to turn the kiss into an act of pure seduction which fired their blood and left them both breathless when they drew apart for a second time.

Sam rested his forehead against hers while his heart raced. He could feel the shudder that worked its way through her body and his arms tightened as he was overcome by tenderness.

'It's crazy, isn't it?' he said thickly.

'That it feels as though we've done this a million times before?' Her laughter was soft and filled with wonder. She let her hand rest along his jaw, her calloused fingertips rasping against the roughness of his beard. 'Maybe we knew one another in a past life Sam. A lot of people believe it can happen so who's to say they're wrong?'

It was an oddly appealing thought even though he'd never considered it before. 'Reincarnation? So, who do you think we were in this other life?' he teased as he drew back to look at her. 'A prince and princess? Somebody rich and famous? Or two very ordinary people who lived very ordinary lives?'

'Hmm, speak for yourself, Sam O'Neill. If I'm going to be reincarnated then I intend to have led a very exciting past life.' She sobered suddenly and her eyes were as deep and green as the ocean as they met his. 'All I'm saying is that you can't rule out things happening, no matter how impossible they might appear to be.'

He knew that she wasn't just talking about the idea of reincarnation and his heart ached. He didn't want to hurt her but he couldn't allow her to start believing things which could never happen. 'Holly, I—'

'No.' She covered his mouth with her fingers. 'You don't need to say anything, Sam. I'm not asking for promises, believe me. I like you and I think you like me. Let's just accept what we have for however long we have it. Think about it, won't you?'

She kissed him lightly on the mouth then let him go. He rose to his feet with a reluctance he couldn't hide, but she didn't try to persuade him to stay. She must have known as well as he did what would happen and it was too soon for that.

He drove away from the house feeling more confused than ever. Life had been so simple a week ago. Then his future had been clearly mapped out, all the i's dotted and the t's crossed. Now he no longer knew what he wanted or if he was doing the right thing. He was deeply attracted to Holly and it was obvious that she wasn't indifferent to him. She made him feel things he'd never believed possible before, made him think things which would have been unthinkable in the past. But what did it mean?

Was he falling in love with her?

Could she be falling in love with him?

What difference would it make to his life if the answer to either of those questions was yes?

It was that last question that scared him most of all.

'A right to-do there was. The whole road was out, listening to their carryings-on.'

Peg Ryan, who cleaned at the surgery, squirted polish onto the coffee-table. The surgery had been closed the previous day for the bank holiday. Sam was coming through the door early on Tuesday morning when he caught the tail-end of the conversation and he paused, wondering what had been going on.

'My Benny was round there playing but he came running back home. Right upset he was, too—' Peg suddenly realised that she had added to her audience. 'Oh, mornin', Dr O'Neill. I was just telling Holly about what happened on Sunday. There was a right old rumpus at the Jacksons' house. Barry's sister has been staying there and her husband came round, kicking up a real fuss when she wouldn't go back home with him.'

'Really?' Sam queried. 'I hope nobody was hurt.'

'No. Oh, there was a lot of argy-bargy, and Barry threatened to thump this other fellow, but one of the neighbours said he was calling the police so Tracey's husband went storming off.' Peg lowered her voice. 'I heard as he'd been in trouble with the police before so I don't suppose he wanted to be around if they turned up.'

'Probably not,' Sam agreed. 'Was Benny all right?'

'Oh, yes. He was upset, mind, kept asking why that man had said horrible things to him. I just told him to take no notice and stay away from the Jacksons' while that Tracey is there. I mean, anyone can see that Benny's not as he should be, but it's downright nasty, calling him a halfwit.'

Peg picked up her duster and marched off down the corridor. Sam sighed. Benny, Peg's twenty-year-old son, had learning disabilities. He had the mind of a child inside the body of a grown man but that didn't make him immune to such hurtful comments. Holly was obviously of the same opinion.

'Fancy saying such dreadful things to poor Benny,' she said in disgust.

'You can't credit the mentality of some people, can you?' Sam frowned. 'Actually, I wonder if what happened at the Jacksons' had anything to do with that car that ran you off the road. The driver was certainly in a hurry.'

'It might.' She frowned as she considered the idea. 'Still, there's no way of proving it, is there? I'll just have to thank my lucky stars that I got off so lightly.'

'How's the knee now?' Sam asked quietly.

'Oh, fine. You have healing hands, Dr O'Neill.' She laughed softly, her green eyes full of a teasing warmth which sent an answering warmth spreading through his body as he was suddenly transported back to those moments in the kitchen.

He'd spent the past thirty-six hours trying to convince himself that it had meant nothing. They were two young healthy adults who found one another attractive—that was all there was to it. But he knew he had as much hope of convincing himself of that as he had of flying to the moon!

'Morning. How's things with you two?' Abbie came bustling into the surgery.

Sam turned to her with a smile that held a tinge of relief. He had to stop letting his mind wander along paths which could lead nowhere. He was leaving at the end of September and that was a fact. Everything else was pure fantasy.

'Fine, thanks. How about you? Oh, have you heard how the Delaneys' son is doing, by the way?' he asked as an afterthought.

'No.' Abbie made a great production out of opening her case and rooting through its contents. 'Damn, where did I put that notebook?' she muttered, steadfastly avoiding his eyes.

He took the hint and didn't pursue the subject. It was obvious that she didn't want to talk about Nick Delaney. The telephone started ringing just then with the first calls of the day so he turned to go to his room then stopped when Holly called to him.

'Sam, Harvey Walsh is on the phone. He sounds in a real panic. He wants to know if you can go over there straight away.'

'Is it Helen again?' he asked, going back to the desk.

'Yes. Evidently, she's had another fall.'

'Tell Harvey I'll be there as soon as I can.' He glanced at his watch as she passed on the message and grimaced. 'Looks like I'm going to miss the start of morning surgery.'

'Can't be helped.' Abbie frowned. 'Something is going to have to be done about that situation soon, Sam. Helen must be persuaded to accept help.'

'Maybe I can get through to her this morning.' He turned to Holly as she put down the receiver. 'Can you tell everyone what's happened? And tell them that I'll be back as fast as I can.'

'Not too fast, Sam. We don't want you having an accident as well.'

He was warmed by her concern, so much so that he tried to make light of it. 'Worried that you might need to return the favour and patch me up?'

'That doesn't worry me in the slightest, not after Sunday.' She returned his smile with one that sent a shiver right down his spine. The phone rang once again and she went to answer it while he took a steadying breath.

'I'd ask what that was all about, only it's *far* more interesting letting my imagination run riot!'

Abbie's teasing laughter followed him from the surgery. He wished he could share her amusement but he was having trouble with his own imagination.

He recited the facts, hoping they'd put a dampener on the pictures that had sprung to mind.

He was leaving in a few weeks' time.

He was going to be thousands of miles away in Africa.

It certainly wasn't the right time to get involved...

It didn't do one little bit of good!

CHAPTER SEVEN

'AM I GLAD to see you, Dr O'Neill!' Harvey Walsh opened the car door as Sam switched off the engine.

'How is Helen?' he asked, quickly lifting his case out of the back and following Harvey inside the house.

'I don't know. She says that she's all right now but when I found her in the yard she couldn't even stand up. I got one of the lads to help me carry her upstairs then I didn't know what to do for the best, whether to phone for an ambulance or ring the surgery. And Helen kept saying as she didn't want me calling anybody.

'I thought if there was anyone she'd listen to it might be you,' Harvey explained worriedly, leading the way upstairs and opening the door to a large sunny bedroom with sloping eaves at either end.

Helen was sitting in a chair by the window. She looked round as the door opened, although she didn't acknowledge Sam in any way. He frowned as he saw the start she gave as he put his case on the bed. Was there something wrong with her eyesight as well as everything else?

'What are you doing out of bed, love?' Harvey demanded, but she ignored the question.

'I thought I told you I didn't need to see the doctor, Harvey,' she said sharply. 'What point is there in dragging him all the way out here when there's nothing wrong with me?'

'Harvey said that you collapsed in the yard,' Sam said easily, going over to her. He deliberately stood a little to one side and could tell immediately that Helen was having trouble focusing on him.

'I just tripped up and winded myself, that's all. I'm perfectly fine, I tell you.' She tried to stand up then sank back onto the chair. It was obvious that she wasn't as well as she was claiming to be.

'Well, seeing as I'm here now, why don't you let me give you the once-over?' Sam suggested. 'It will set Harvey's mind at rest if nothing else.'

'If you must. But it's a lot of fuss about nothing, so far as I'm concerned.' She gave in with ill grace and sat stiffly while he listened to her heart and lungs then took her pulse.

'Mmm, that all appears to be in order. I'll just check your blood pressure in case that's the reason for these falls you keep having.'

Helen's blood pressure proved to be perfectly normal as well. Sam put the sphygmomanometer back in his case. 'No problem there either. Now, if I can just check your eyes.'

He took his ophthalmoscope from his case and bent down to examine her eyes, frowning as he found definite signs of nystagmus. He was immediately reminded of what Holly had suggested as this kind of involuntary eye movement could often be attributed to alcohol abuse.

'Do you know what's wrong, Dr O'Neill?' Harvey held up his hand when Helen went to speak. 'No, love. You can tell me till you're blue in the face, but *I* know that you haven't been yourself lately. This needs getting to the bottom of once and for all.'

'There's nothing wrong with me!' Helen struggled

to her feet and glared at her husband. 'As for you, Dr O'Neill, all I can say is thank you very much for coming but Harvey should never have phoned you in the first place. Now, if you don't mind, I have things to do.'

Harvey stared after her as she left the room. 'I can't seem to make her see sense. I'm telling you that if you'd seen her an hour ago then you'd also be convinced there was something wrong, Dr O'Neill.'

'I'm sure you're right. But unless Helen is willing to co-operate there is very little I can do.' Sam put the ophthalmoscope back in his bag and snapped the locks shut. He wondered how best to phrase his next question but there was no easy way to go about it. 'How much alcohol does Helen drink throughout a week?'

'Alcohol?' Harvey stared at him as though he'd taken leave of his senses. 'You're not trying to say that's what the problem is, surely? It's ridiculous! Apart from the odd glass of sherry at Christmas, she never touches a drop from one year to the next.'

'Are you sure? Look, I know this probably sounds crazy to you, but a lot of the symptoms she's been exhibiting could stem from alcohol dependency—the clumsiness and frequent accidents, the inability to focus properly which was so obvious when I arrived. Even the slurred speech which you yourself remarked on.'

Harvey was shaking his head even before Sam had finished. 'No. I tell you you're barking up the wrong tree entirely, Doctor.'

'Maybe. But bear it in mind, Harvey, won't you? In the meantime, I want you to call me if there are any further developments. And if you can persuade Helen to come in to see me so we can run some tests, all the better.'

'I'll try. But you can forget about it being drink that's causing the trouble, Dr O'Neill. Helen's the last person on earth who would take to the bottle.'

Harvey sounded insulted by the mere suggestion. Sam wasn't surprised. A lot of people saw alcohol dependency as something to be ashamed of rather than an illness. They left the room together and walked back along the landing. They were just passing one of the bedrooms when a querulous voice called to them.

'Is that the doctor you've got there, son?'

'Yes, Mum. It's Dr O'Neill,' Harvey replied, opening the door so that his mother could see who was there. The old lady beckoned to Sam.

'Come in, come in, lad. Don't stand there where I can hardly see you.'

Sam hid a smile as he went into the room. At ninety years of age the old lady had earned the right to be a trifle imperious. 'Hello, Mrs Walsh, how are you doing? You're looking well, I must say.'

'Oh, mustn't grumble. No point, is there? Folk don't want to hear about your ailments when you get to my age.' She gave a cackling laugh. 'Still, seeing as you're here, I wonder if you'd just take a look at this hip, Doctor.'

'Certainly.' Sam frowned as he went over to the bed. 'Is it the hip you broke a month or so back? I thought the operation to replace the joint had been successful?'

'Oh, it's been all right but I'd still like you to take

a look.' Mrs Walsh looked at her son. 'I'd like a cup of tea if you've nothing else to do, Harvey.'

Harvey sighed. 'I'll go and put the kettle on, then. How about you, Dr O'Neill?'

'Not for me, thanks.' Sam waited until Harvey had left the room then turned to the old lady again. 'Now, if you'd just like to show me what the problem is…'

'Oh, that was just an excuse to have a word with you without Harvey hearing,' she explained quickly. 'There's nowt wrong with this new hip. It hasn't given me a bit of trouble. No, it's Helen I wanted to speak to you about. They think I don't know what's going on, being stuck in this room all the time, but I'm neither deaf nor daft and not much passes me by. I have my own view on what's wrong with her.'

Sam sat down on the side of the bed. 'Have you? Then I'd like to hear it because something needs to be done about this situation.'

'Helen's scared, you see. That's why she's pretending nothing is wrong with her.'

'But what is she scared of? We only want to help her.' He was at a loss to understand. He heard Mrs Walsh sigh heavily.

'I've lived in this town all my life, Dr O'Neill, so there's not much which has gone on over the years I don't know about. I remember Helen's mother, although she died when Helen was just a child. She had a brain tumour or so I heard at the time. I don't know the ins and outs out of it, but Helen's father walked out on the family. I suppose he couldn't cope. Helen and her brother were brought up by relatives after their mother died.'

'I see.' Sam frowned as he tried to link what he'd been told to what was happening. 'So you think that

Helen's afraid she might have what her mother had? And that Harvey will react the way her father did?'

'Yes. She was only a youngster at the time and it must have left a lasting impression on her—' Mrs Walsh broke off as Harvey appeared with a cup of tea. 'And about time, too. That's the trouble with being old—folk forget about you.'

'We don't get much chance to forget about *you*, Mum!' Harvey retorted, putting the cup down within easy reach of the old lady.

'I make sure you don't. Well, thank you, Doctor. I'm sorry if I kept you.'

Sam took the hint. 'Oh, any time you're worried, Mrs Walsh, just get in touch with the surgery. One of us will pop out to see you.'

He left the old lady drinking her tea. Helen was in the kitchen and she didn't say anything as he passed the door. Harvey saw him out to his car, still looking worried.

Sam tried his best to reassure him but knew he'd failed. It made him all the more determined to make Helen see sense, although it wasn't going to be easy if Mrs Walsh's suspicions were correct. What had happened in Helen's childhood had left its mark—as it did on so many people.

Would he have been so afraid of commitment if his childhood had been different? he found himself wondering. It was hard to tell.

There was no time to speak to anyone about Helen Walsh when he got back to the surgery as there was a backlog of patients to catch up with. He finished way after the time he should have done and then there was an antenatal clinic that afternoon which he was rostered for. That was followed by evening surgery and another round of patients to see, by which time he'd forgotten all about the problem.

It was as he was on his way home that night that he remembered, and he pulled into the kerb as he tried to decide what to do.

He could leave it until the morning to speak to one of his colleagues but they were always so busy that there was no guarantee he'd get the chance even then. Something had to be done about this situation soon. He debated going back to have a word with Elizabeth but suddenly remembered that she'd mentioned going for a fitting for her wedding dress that night. James was on call so it didn't seem fair to bother him, which left David.

He set off towards David's house, trying to quell the rush of anticipation at the thought that Holly would be there. This was strictly a professional visit, he told himself sternly, but it did little to suppress the feeling as he drew up in the drive. He got out to knock on the door then paused as a waft of fragrant smoke drifted from the back garden accompanied by the sound of laughter.

Sam followed the path round the house and found everyone except Holly clustered around the barbecue. Laura suddenly spotted him and came hurrying over to kiss him on the cheek.

'Sam! How lovely. Come and join the party. There's tons of food.'

'I don't want to interrupt—' he began, but Laura cut him off with a laugh.

'Don't be silly. Of course you aren't interrupting. Now, what will you have to eat? There's burgers and sausages and if the chef ever gets his act together, there might even be steak.' She shot a teasing glance at David, who shook the long-handled fork he was using to turn the steaks at her.

'Slave-driver! You wouldn't believe that behind that gentle exterior beats a heart of steel.' David grinned as he turned to Sam. 'Anyway, it's nice to see you. Is this a social call or what?'

'Actually I wanted a word with you, but I can see this isn't the best moment,' he explained ruefully.

'Oh, don't worry about— Oh, good, you've brought Sam a plate, have you, darling? Can you just sort him out while I keep my eyes on these steaks? My life won't be worth living if I let them burn.'

'What would you like, Sam?'

He swung round at the sound of that husky voice, feeling heat suffuse him as he found Holly standing behind him. His eyes skimmed from the top of her honey-brown hair to the tips of her bare feet while he felt every cell in his body respond with purely masculine appreciation.

That sleeveless yellow vest top clung to her slender body in the most enticing way while the skimpy cut-off jeans simply emphasised the length of her shapely legs. He would have needed to be a monk to remain immune to the sight of her so that it took him all his time to reply in a voice which was halfway normal. Even then he was sure that she'd guessed what was going through his mind.

'Oh, I don't mind. Anything will do, a burger, sausage…whatever's easiest.'

'Right you are.'

She bent over the barbecue and took a selection off the hot metal grill. Handing him the plate, she ran her fingers down the seat of her shorts to wipe away any splatters of grease. He only just managed to contain his groan. The thought of how it would be to let his own hands follow the same route over that delectable derrière was too much for any red-blooded male!

He took a rather unwary bite of sausage and almost choked as he discovered how hot it was.

'Careful!' Holly thumped him on the back as he began to splutter. She took the plate out of his hand and set it down on a nearby table, watching in concern as he wiped his streaming eyes. 'Are you OK?'

'I think so.' He grimaced, feeling like the world's biggest idiot. 'I didn't realise that sausage was so hot,' he added lamely.

'Hmm, that's the funny thing about barbecues—the food does tend to be hot.' Her eyes shone as she teased him and he couldn't help laughing.

'All right, you don't need to rub it in.' He pushed his handkerchief back in his pocket and picked up his plate again, taking an exaggeratedly dainty bite this time.

'That's better. Now you're getting the idea.' She quickly filled a plate for herself then led him away from the barbecue to where some lawn chairs had been arranged under an old pear tree and motioned him to sit down. 'I didn't know you were coming tonight, Sam. Dad never mentioned it.'

'I only dropped in to have a word with him about Helen Walsh, to be honest. I needed to get his advice on what I should do about something I found out today.' He sat down beside her and made himself comfortable in the old chair. It was growing dark and this part of the garden was sheltered by the overhang of the tree so that they seemed to be cut off from the others.

He heard Mike laugh then Emily's high-pitched squeal and glanced round to see what was happening, smiling as he saw Mike swing his little sister into the air and race off towards the house with her over his shoulder.

'Looks like they're having fun,' he observed, unaware of the wistful note in his voice.

'Did you ever do things like this when you were a child, Sam?'

He heard the curiosity in her voice and knew that it was prompted by a real desire to learn more about him. It made him a little uneasy. Opening up about his past was something he had always avoided and it was hard to change old habits.

'Not really. I was an only child for starters, which made a difference,' he said carefully.

'It must have done. But how about friends? I imagine you had a lot of those,' she said, watching him closely as she picked up her burger and bit into it.

'Some. Unfortunately, my parents moved around a lot so it was a case of making new friends, then making more when we went to a new town to live.' He shrugged, a little surprised at how easy it was to tell her now that he'd overcome that first hurdle.

'The longest time I spent in any one place was when I was put into foster care after my parents died, and even then I didn't remain with the same family for the whole time. I had five different placements in as many years so I never really had chance to settle down anywhere.'

'I can't imagine what that must have been like,' she said quietly. There was compassion in her eyes as she looked at him, mingled with regret. 'I was so lucky because Mum and Dad were always here for

me. It makes me ashamed when I think how I be-
haved after Mum died and compare it to how you
had to learn to cope so young.'

'Everyone deals with a problem his or her own
way.' Sam put his plate down on the grass beside
him. He took a deep breath, wondering if it was wise
to carry on this conversation. He'd never examined
his motives for the way he'd run his life up till now,
and yet suddenly he could understand it so much
more clearly. 'I've never put down roots anywhere,
probably because of my childhood. I'm so used to
moving on that it's become a habit, I expect.'

'But that could change, Sam. One day you could
meet someone and know that you want to stay with
her.' Her eyes lifted to his and he felt his heart contract as he saw the entreaty they held.

'I don't know, Holly. How can I? All my life I've
shied away from the idea of commitment. It wouldn't
be fair to any woman to make promises I might not
be able to keep. In a month's time I fly out to Africa,
and who knows where I'll go after that? It…it simply
isn't the right time to start making decisions.'

'I see.' She stood up abruptly, a smile fixed to her
mouth which didn't disguise the hurt he could see in
her eyes. 'Then all I can say is that I hope you'll be
happy whatever you choose to do.'

She moved away to join the others. Sam sighed as
he watched her. It *wasn't* the right time to start making changes to his life. He knew that but it didn't
make it any easier to know he was right…

'I hope you're going to have seconds, Sam, otherwise we'll be eating leftovers for the next week.'

He tried to shake off the feeling of melancholy as
Laura sat down beside him. 'In that case, I'd better

get a move on and finish this little lot,' he said with forced brightness. Picking up his plate, he set about the food although he really wasn't hungry. Someone laughed and the fork stopped midway to his mouth as he recognised the sound immediately. Even in the middle of a crowded room he'd be able to pick out Holly's laughter without the slightest hesitation, he realised, his heart aching with frustration because it was so pointless to feel like this.

'There is a way round most problems if you're determined enough to find it, Sam.' Laura spoke softly but she claimed his attention at once.

'Sorry?'

She smiled as she looked deliberately at Holly, who was standing at the far end of the garden. 'I'm just saying that most situations aren't black and white. You have to be willing to compromise but there's usually a solution to even the biggest problem.'

He felt his face grow hot as he understood what she meant. Was he really as transparent as all that? He took a deep breath then suddenly realised there was no point in lying.

'I'm leaving in a few weeks' time,' he said flatly. 'I don't think there's enough time to work out a compromise, especially when I'm not sure it's what either of us want.'

'Then maybe you should decide that before you do anything, Sam. I wouldn't like to see either you or Holly getting hurt.' Laura glanced up as David came to join them. 'Ah, the chef. My compliments, maestro. That steak was delicious—especially those crunchy black bits round the edges.'

'Wretched woman!' David swatted her rear end as

she got up from the chair, grinning as she stuck her tongue out at him. He sat down with a sigh as she wandered off. 'I think I'll stick to doctoring from now on. It's a lot less stressful than labouring over a hot grill. Anyway, what did you want to speak to me about, Sam? Is there a problem?'

It was a relief to focus on something other than the situation between him and Holly. Sam quickly ran through everything he'd learned about Helen Walsh that morning. 'I wasn't sure what to do, or if there was anything I *could* do,' he concluded.

'I see what you mean.' David frowned. 'It's a bit of a predicament. As Helen hasn't said anything herself it could be construed as breaking a patient's confidence if you mention this to Harvey.'

'That's what I thought. If Helen had wanted her husband to know then she'd have told him. And, of course, we could be completely wrong and jumping to conclusions.'

'We could, but it all seems to fit—' David stopped as the phone started ringing. Mike ran in to answer it and came back a few seconds later.

'It's Mr Farnsworth, Dad. He wants a word with you.'

'No rest for the wicked.' David heaved himself out of the chair and headed into the house. Sam got up and carried his plate back to the table. There was no sign of Holly so he could only assume that she'd gone inside. Maybe it was time he took his leave. After all there was little he could say to make things better between them. He couldn't and wouldn't make any promises he might come to regret. He cared too much about her to do that.

'Well, that's all we need.' David came back, looking worried. 'One of the kids has gone missing from the Outward Bound centre. Ian discovered he was gone about fifteen minutes ago when he went to the sanatorium to check on him.'

'Did you say he was in the san.?' Sam queried. 'It wouldn't be young Jason by any chance?'

'Yes. Ian said you'd been over there to see him on Sunday. Evidently the boy didn't take kindly to being confined to bed. Ian has had Jason's friends in the office but they won't admit to knowing where he's gone.'

'Has Ian contacted the rescue services?' Laura asked in concern.

'He has but they're already out, looking for a party of hill walkers who failed to return to base. Ian's getting a team together to go and look for the boy and wanted to know if we'd help,' David explained.

'Of course,' Sam agreed immediately. 'Where are we meeting? At the centre?'

'Yes. In half an hour's time.'

'Then I'd better get off back home and change,' Sam said at once. 'I'll see you down there.'

He drove straight home, stopping only long enough to change into hiking gear and pack a few essentials. Although it was a mild night, he'd lived in the area long enough to know that the weather could change very rapidly and that going up onto the hills unprepared was asking for trouble.

Everyone was gathered in front of the building when he arrived. Ian Farnsworth split them into groups. 'We need to cover as much ground as possible so we'll work on a buddy system. It isn't ideal but as long as each pair has a flare and either a radio or mobile phone as a means of communication there shouldn't be a problem.'

Ian began pairing people off and the drive quickly emptied. Sam was near the back so he waited for his turn. He couldn't see any sign of David until a car drew up. He just had a second to realise that both Mike and Holly were with him before Ian pointed towards him. 'You go with Holly, Sam. One of the lads will show you which area you're to cover and make sure you have everything you need. Now, David, you take Mike…'

Sam didn't hear anything more. He turned and followed Holly to where one of the staff was dishing out ordinance survey sheets of the area. Each section to be covered had been circled in red and numbered. Holly checked the directions she was given then turned to him with a thin smile.

'Ready? Looks as though you're stuck with me, whether you like it or not.'

CHAPTER EIGHT

'HOLD on a minute. I need to check our bearings.'

Sam dropped the rucksack onto the ground while he stopped to check the compass. Night had fallen completely now and the darkness was barely broken by a thin sliver of moon, peeping through the gathering clouds. They'd been walking for almost an hour and Holly had said hardly a word.

Sure that they were heading in the right direction, he put the compass back in his pocket then unfastened the bag and took out a can of cola. 'Want some?' he offered, popping the tab and holding it towards her.

'No, thanks.' She walked to the end of the outcrop of rocks and stared down the valley, her back turned deliberately towards him. Sam bit back a sigh. He had the most ungentlemanly urge to shake her but he wasn't sure that would be the most sensible thing to do so he decided to try reason instead.

'Look, Holly, I know you're annoyed—'

'Who said I'm annoyed?' She swung round, defiance in every line of her posture. 'Don't flatter yourself, Sam O'Neill. Frankly, I don't give a damn what you do.'

'Then why are you acting like a...a spoiled brat who's having a tantrum?' Reason disappeared as he felt his own temper stir to life.

'Spoiled brat! I don't have to stay here and listen to that.' She started to storm off then suddenly remembered where they were. He saw her lips twitch as the sheer ridiculousness of the situation struck her.

'Not the best place to make a dignified exit from, is it?' she said with a wry chuckle, glancing back at him.

He laughed softly as he went over to join her. Propping himself against the rock face, he sipped at the frothing cola can. 'I've seen better,' he teased.

'I'm sure you have,' she agreed dryly. She leaned back against the rocks with a sigh. 'I'm sorry, Sam. The last thing I want is for us to argue.'

'Me, too.' He cupped the can in his hand, watching as the clouds turned to black lace as the moon slid behind them. 'The last thing I want is to hurt you in any way, Holly.'

'I know that. It's just that…'

'Just what? Tell me,' he prompted when she stopped.

'That I don't understand why you won't accept I meant what I said. I'm not asking for promises, Sam. I…I'd just like the chance for us to get to know one another better.'

'Oh, Holly, if it were only that simple.' He put the can down on the ground and drew her into his arms. He nuzzled his face against her hair, breathing in the fragrance of the shampoo she used.

'Why can't it be that simple? Surely it can be as simple or…or as complicated as we make it?'

It was that slight hesitation which worried him most of all. He tipped his head back and stared into her beautiful face. It was so tempting to agree to what she was suggesting but he had to be sensible—and make her see sense as well.

'I'm going to be in Africa for two whole years.

And after that I have no idea where I'll be or what
I'll be doing. It just isn't the right time to get into a
relationship at this point. You must see that, surely?'

'What I see, Sam, is that you've made up your
mind and have no intention of being swayed by anything I say.' The sadness in her voice cut him deeply.
He struggled to find something to say but there was
nothing he could think of. They seemed to be going
round in circles but he knew in his heart that he was
right.

He picked up the haversack as she moved away
and started along the path once more. They carried
on for another half-hour, concentrating on the search.
It was a relief because it was impossible to sort out
this situation when they both had such opposing
views. Every five minutes they stopped and shouted
Jason's name but there was no response. The clouds
had thickened fast, blotting out any sign of the moon.
It was no surprise when it began to rain, the first few
drops turning quickly into a downpour.

'Here, let's shelter behind these rocks while I
check to see if there's any news.' Sam moved into
the lee of the hill and used his mobile phone to call
the centre. Ian's wife, Barbara, was manning the radio and phones, and she quickly informed him that
there was no news of the boy. Several groups had
returned to base already and were waiting for Ian to
get back and issue fresh instructions. He briefly con-
firmed their position then ended the call.

'No luck as yet?' Holly asked, drawing her hood
further over her head as the rain pelted down on
them.

'No, no sign of him.' Sam sighed as he tucked the
phone back in the bag and glanced at the sky.

'Heaven knows how he'll fare in this weather. I know it isn't winter but on a night like this he'll soon get chilled. More people die from exposure during relatively mild weather than any other time because they're unprepared for it.'

'How much more ground have we got to cover?' Holly peered over his shoulder as he spread out the map and showed her where they were. 'Just that section which backs onto Isaac Shepherd's land?'

'That's it.' He refolded the map and slipped it back into his pocket. 'Come on. We'd better get it over and done with.'

It was a miserable half-hour. The driving rain made it difficult to see where they were going so that there was always the danger that they might pass by the boy and not spot him. Sam switched on the torch so that its light would be a beacon for anyone out on the hills, but by the time Isaac Shepherd's farm came into view they'd given up all hope of finding young Jason.

Holly dashed rain off her face as they stopped on the hill above the farmhouse. 'Well, that seems to be that, doesn't it?' she said glumly.

'It does—' He broke off as a noisy barking broke the silence. Wherever the dog was, it was setting up a real furore. He peered towards the farmhouse and saw a light moving around in the farmyard. 'I wonder what's going on down there.'

'Do you think we should go and take a look?' She sounded worried. 'I believe old Isaac has been ill recently—a heart attack, wasn't it? I wouldn't like to think of him having to deal with an intruder all by himself.'

'Me neither,' Sam said grimly, setting off down

the hill as fast as conditions allowed. Holly was some way behind him when he reached the yard and he came to a dead stop as a dog suddenly came round the side of the barn, growling menacingly.

'Who's there?' A querulous voice demanded before Isaac appeared, holding aloft an oil lamp.

'It's me, Mr Shepherd,' Sam said quickly as the dog took a threatening step towards him, its teeth bared in a snarl. 'Sam O'Neill.' He glanced round as Holly arrived, holding up his hand to warn her to stop. 'And I've got Holly Ross with me.'

'Dr Ross's lass?' Isaac held the lantern a bit higher. 'What on earth are you doing out here at this time of the night, the pair of you?'

'There's a young boy missing from the Outward Bound centre and we're part of the search party,' he explained, keeping a wary eye on the collie, which was crouched ready to spring.

'I see.' Isaac glanced at the dog. 'All right, Tess. Friends.'

The dog jumped up, her tail wagging furiously as she came to greet them. Sam laughed as he bent down and patted her silky head.

'That's some guard dog you've got there. She wasn't going to let us within ten yards of the house unless you gave the word.'

'Aye, she's a good lass, right enough.' Issac fondly stroked the dog's head as she went back to him. He frowned as he glanced down at the old-fashioned wool dressing-gown he was wearing beneath a shabby weatherproof jacket. 'I wonder if it was you Tess was barking at just now. She was making a terrible racket, which is what woke me up.'

'I don't think so.' Sam glanced at Holly, who

shook her head. 'We were up on the hill when she started barking so I don't think it was us who upset her.'

'Then what did?' Isaac looked grimly towards the barn. 'Maybe it was that dog which has been coming round here, ugly great grey beast it is. Looks more like a donkey than any dog I've seen. If it's been round here tonight after my Tess…'

Sam saw Holly look at him and just managed to keep his face straight. The description fit Peebody to a T, although neither of them were prepared to tell Isaac that. They followed the old man to the barn, both of them wondering what they'd find as he pushed open the door. The smell of clean hay and straw met them, mixed with the scent of rust from the old farming implements which were stored there.

'I'll have its hide if it's in here…' Isaac held the lantern aloft as he peered into the shadows. There was a rustling from the far corner and he hurried forward as Tess started barking again, prodding the heap of dry straw with his foot. 'Out with you! Come on, out!'

Sam wasn't sure who was most surprised when the straw parted and a boy's face peered out. 'Jason! How on earth did you get there?'

'It weren't hard.' Jason shrugged as he stood up and brushed straw off himself. He was wearing jeans and a T-shirt and it was obvious that he was wringing wet. His bright red hair stuck up in a cow-lick at the front, the rash which peppered his cheeks looking all the more startling in the glow from the lantern.

Sam could see that he was shivering violently de-spite his bravado so he quickly took off his jacket and draped it around the child's shoulders. 'We need to get you out of those wet clothes for starters,' he said, then glanced at Holly. 'Can you phone Ian and tell him what's happened?'

'Of course.' She went out of the barn to make the call and came back a couple of minutes later. 'Ian's on his way—he shouldn't be long.' She looked at the shivering child and turned to Isaac. 'Is there any chance we could come inside to wait, Mr Shepherd? Jason needs to get warmed up a bit.'

'Aye, I suppose so,' Isaac conceded grudgingly, and led the way back to the house. As was the case in many of the outlying farmhouses, the fire was kept burning day and night to provide heating and cooking facilities. Isaac stirred the embers with a huge old poker then threw on another log from the box beside the hearth. 'That should catch in a moment or two. Put the kettle on to boil, lass, while I find the lad something dry to wear.'

Within ten minutes they were all sitting round the fire, drinking tea, with Jason warmly muffled up in an old jumper of Issac's which smelled strongly of mothballs.

'What a pong!' Jason wrinkled his nose in disgust. 'It's wicked.'

'Wicked?' Isaac shook his head. 'Sometimes wonder if I'm on the same planet as these youngsters.' He turned a gimlet eye on the boy. 'Get that tea down you and stop moaning, lad. Here's some biscuits to go with it, and don't go slipping bits to the dog neither.'

He sat down, pretending not to notice when Jason broke off a piece of biscuit and slyly passed it to an appreciative Tess. Sam hid his smile. Isaac was a

character all right but he had a heart of gold under-
neath that gruff exterior.

'Right, then, Jason, let's hear it. How did you get
here? It must be a good ten miles from the centre to
the farm.'

Jason crammed a whole biscuit into his mouth then
spoke with his mouth full. Some of his perkiness was
coming back now that he was warm and dry again.
'I hid in the back of a van, one of those delivery
vans from that pottery place. It came to the centre
just after tea tonight and I got in the back while the
driver wasn't looking.'

'That'll be my son Frank's van,' Isaac exclaimed.
'He told me as he'd been delivering some new crock-
ery to that Outward Bound place before he called in
to see me tonight.'

'I thought it would be going miles away from here,
some place where there'd be a cinema and stuff like
that,' Jason explained in obvious disgust. 'When I
heard the driver saying he was going back to town I
got out. I walked along the road for a bit, thinking
that I'd get a lift, but there weren't any cars. It got
dark and then it started raining so I came back and
hid in the barn.'

'And that's when Tess must have heard you,' Sam
finished. 'Anyway, it was a stupid thing to do. Quite
apart from the fact that you could have been seriously injured, wandering about on your own, you've
caused a lot of trouble tonight. Mr Farnsworth is not
going to be pleased, I can tell you.'

Jason looked suitably contrite although Sam
doubted that would last long. He caught Holly's eye
and saw by her expression that she was of the same
opinion. Ian arrived not long after that to collect them

and they drove back to the centre. Sam went in and gave the boy a quick check, but apart from his temperature being a little higher than normal he seemed none the worse for his adventures. A good night's sleep should soon put him right.

'Thanks a lot, both of you,' Ian said as he saw them out to the car. 'Young Jason got off very lightly tonight but he might not have been half so lucky if the weather had been really bad.'

Sam sighed as they drove away. 'At least it was a happy ending of sorts, although Jason might not think so.'

Holly grinned. 'Oh, I'm sure he'll make the most of it. I can just imagine him regaling his friends with his adventures, can't you?'

'Yes, unfortunately. I have a feeling that it will take more than that to put young Jason down.' Sam laughed then just managed to stifle the yawn that crept up on him. 'Excuse me. I think I'm more than ready for my bed. How about you?'

'Oh, me, too! I'm shattered.'

They kept up a desultory conversation as they drove back to town. It was almost twelve-thirty when they drew up in front of Holly's house. Sam yawned again as his body clock reminded him he was missing out on sleep.

'I must be getting old. A night out on those hills and I'm completely bushed.' He gave her a wry smile, his senses stirring as she smiled back.

'It's been a long night, hasn't it, Sam?' she said softly.

'Yes,' he replied, although he was barely conscious of what he was saying at that moment. His eyes ran over the delicate features of her face with a hunger he couldn't disguise, and he saw her eyes darken. He wasn't sure which of them moved first but suddenly his arms were around her and hers were around him…

Her lips were so soft yet they returned the pressure of his with equal fervour. Sam's heart leapt as he felt the eagerness with which she returned his kiss. He drew her closer, letting his lips follow the contours of her face from temple to jaw before coming to rest on that delectable pulse in her neck which was beating out its own frenzied message. Feeling it throbbing away, it set up an answering throb in his body which was impossible to ignore.

He framed her face with his hands as he kissed her again, his lips moving over hers with a delicacy that wrung a moan from her. She let her head drop to his shoulder when he let her go, her breath coming in fast little spurts that matched the laboured sound of his own breathing.

'Do you still think you are right, Sam?'

He knew what she meant, of course, and his heart ached. He pulled her back into his arms, feeling her softness melting against him, a perfect match for his own body.

What harm could there be in them enjoying one another's company as long as they both understood the rules? the voice of temptation whispered. Wouldn't it be something to look back on, a memory to cherish when he went away? Suddenly he was beyond resisting when it was what both his mind and body wanted so much.

He kissed her again then let her go, and his eyes were very dark as they centred on her upturned face. 'Do you think we can handle it, Holly?'

She must have heard the uncertainty in his voice because her reply was quick and fervent. 'Yes. We both know what we're doing, Sam.'

Did they, though? He felt a momentary qualm because he wasn't sure either of them fully understood the consequences. And yet, with her looking at him with such conviction, it wasn't hard to vanquish his doubts. 'Then would you like to come to dinner with me tomorrow night?'

'I'd like that very much. Thank you.' She kissed him swiftly on the lips then opened the car door. He waited until she'd gone inside then drove home. Letting himself into the house, he went straight upstairs and got ready for bed. Switching off the light, he lay in the darkness while his mind raced in circles, always coming back to Holly and how he felt about her.

It wasn't just physical attraction he felt for her but so much more. He wanted to be there when she needed him, to take care of her, but was he capable of that sort of commitment? He had no way of knowing because it was something he'd never done before. The thought of holding someone's future happiness in his hands scared him…

He sighed as he realised that his racing mind was off down a fresh path. He'd asked her out to dinner, not proposed marriage! Both of them understood the rules…

Oh, yes? that tormenting voice taunted, taking a different track this time just to confuse him even more. And wasn't there a saying about rules being made to be broken?

Oh, hell!

*   *   *

Sam arrived at the surgery the next morning to find the place in a state of chaos. The phone was ringing away but nobody was making any attempt to answer it. They were all gathered in the staffroom, looking incredibly sombre.

'What's going on?' he asked James, *sotto voce*, as he went in to join them.

'Elizabeth had some bad news this morning. Her father has suffered another heart attack. Her sister rang to tell her that he's in hospital. Apparently, his doctors have said that the next twenty-four hours are critical,' James explained equally quietly.

'Oh, no! That was the last thing Liz was expecting. She was only saying the other day that her father would be home soon and that he was looking forward to the wedding,' Sam replied, saddened by the news. Although he hadn't worked with Charles Allen for very long, he'd liked the older man and had admired his skill and dedication.

He went over to Elizabeth and hugged her, 'James just told me about your father, Liz. I'm really sorry.'

'Thank you.' She tried to smile but it was obvious how upset she was. 'I just wish I knew what to do for the best...'

'I don't think there's any question about that, darling.' James slipped his arm around her shoulders. 'You must fly out to Australia immediately. I'm going to get straight onto the airlines to see if I can find you a seat.'

'Oh, but I couldn't...'

'Of course you can.' James's tone was firm. 'We can manage without you for a couple of weeks. You'd never forgive yourself if you weren't there and something happened.'

'But we're so busy here. And then there's the wedding and everything,' she protested.

'James is right, Liz.' David added his voice to the argument. 'Your father needs you with him at a time like this. Everything else simply has to take second place.'

'And you can always leave a list of things which need to be done,' Abbie put in. 'I'll be happy to sort it all out.'

'Well, I suppose so…' It was obvious that she was being swayed by their arguments. When James muttered something about getting onto it right away she made no further protest. The phone started ringing again and Sam went to answer it, wondering where Holly had got to. There was no sign of her and it wasn't like her to be late.

He took the message then put the phone down just as the door opened. He looked round, expecting it to be Holly, and was startled when Eileen, the receptionist, appeared. 'Hello, what are you doing here? I didn't know you were back from your sister's.'

'No?' Eileen hung her jacket on the peg and smoothed her already immaculate grey hair. 'I did phone Elizabeth last night and told her that I'd be in this morning. My sister is much better so there was no point in my staying with her any longer when there's so much to be done here.'

Sam sighed. 'I see. Unfortunately, Elizabeth had some bad news this morning so it must have slipped her mind.'

He quickly explained the situation to her then went along to his room to get ready for his patients, trying to ignore the little pang of disappointment he felt at not seeing Holly that morning. He shrugged it off by reminding himself that he'd see her that night for dinner. It was something to look forward to.

The chaotic start to the day continued unabated. James managed to get Elizabeth a seat on a flight which was due to leave Heathrow at seven that evening. Allowing for the check-in time, it meant that she had to be in London by five at the latest. She had to miss morning surgery to get ready so they split her list between them with Sam and David taking the bulk of the extra appointments as James was going to drive her down there and needed to leave early.

It entailed a lot of juggling but eventually everything was sorted out. David would do the house calls while Sam took the antenatal clinic and they'd worry about evening surgery when they had to. When Sally Roberts, the midwife, rang to say that she couldn't make it to the clinic to help out, as she was on her way to a delivery, it was just another hiccup in the day.

'We'll manage,' Sam said ruefully. 'We'll have to!'

'Best way to look at it.' David groaned, then suddenly slapped his forehead. 'Damn, I forgot. I'm booked to speak at a dinner tonight—the local farmers' association do. Liz was on call tonight and I told her I'd take over for her but I won't be able to now. I'm sorry to drop it on you like this, Sam, but I don't have any choice. I can't let them down at this late stage.'

'Of course you can't.' He tried to hide his disappointment that he'd have to cancel his date with Holly. 'Don't worry about it.'

He tried to phone Holly as soon as he got a free

moment, to tell her that he'd have to call the evening off, but nobody answered at her house. There was no time to try again as the first expectant mums started arriving.

It was a hectic afternoon but he enjoyed it enormously. As it was still the school holidays several of the women had brought their children with them. Sam found that they were fascinated by their unborn brothers or sisters so he spent a lot of time explaining what he was doing. The most popular part seemed to be when they listened to the new baby's heartbeat. By the time Sophie Jackson appeared for her appointment he was running behind schedule but it couldn't be helped. In his opinion it was important to involve siblings in the arrival of the new baby at every stage.

'Right, Sophie, come and stand on the scales for me so I can check your weight,' he instructed, smiling at the Jacksons' eldest child. Sophie was only just sixteen and the baby hadn't been planned, but she was coping extremely well with the pregnancy.

'That's fine. You seem to be keeping your weight well down. You're what…thirty-four weeks now?'

'Yes. Dr Allen said that I'll have to come to the clinic every week soon,' Sophie replied, stepping off the scales.

'That's right. You'll need to be seen weekly from thirty-six weeks onwards so that we can keep a close eye on you and the baby. Now, have you brought a urine sample with you?' He took the sample and, using a colour-coded test strip, quickly tested it for any signs of diabetes or proteinuria, but once again everything was fine.

'Well, full marks so far. I'll just take your blood

pressure next.' He unrolled the sphygmomanometer's cuff and wrapped it around the girl's arm, frowning as he found that Sophie's blood pressure was a little higher than it should have been. 'Hmm, a bit up on what I'd like it to be. Have you been resting, Sophie? I'm sure Dr Allen has told you how important it is at this stage.'

'I do try but it isn't easy. With Tracey and Katie staying with us, the house is bursting at the seams,' Sophie replied with a sigh. 'They're sharing my room because there isn't anywhere else for them, and Katie wakes up a lot through the night, crying.'

'It must be very difficult,' Sam sympathised. 'How long is your aunt staying?'

'I don't know. It was supposed to be just for a few days but she's got herself this part-time job at the pottery so it looks as though it's going to be a while. I've been looking after Katie while she's at work,' she added.

'Well, you really mustn't do too much. Hypertension can interfere with the blood supply to the placenta and your baby could suffer. You really have to think about yourself first and foremost now,' he advised.

'That's what Billy keeps telling me,' she said, re-ferring to young Billy Murray, the father of her child. 'He wants me to go and stay at his house but I don't know about that. His grandad is OK, but his mum and dad have made it plain how they feel about me.'

Sam sighed, realising what a difficult situation it was for both families. Billy was only a little older than Sophie so it must have been almost as much of shock for his parents as hers. However, his main con-cern had to be Sophie and the baby. 'It must be hard,

Sophie, but you have to make sure that you get enough rest. Have a word with your mum and tell her what I've said. Maybe she can find Tracey somewhere else to stay.'

'I'll try, but I can't see Tracey wanting to live on her own, especially not after the commotion her husband made the other day.' Sophie stood up and grimaced. 'I might find myself taking Billy up on his offer at this rate, although I can't see it working out.'

Clinic finally came to an end, by which time there were patients arriving for evening surgery. Eileen had spent the afternoon phoning around and quite a few of Elizabeth's and James's patients had agreed to reschedule their appointments, but there were still extra people to see. They were all glad when they were able to lock up and go home at last.

Sam opened his front door, feeling tired beyond belief. He'd phoned Holly and had left a message with Mike as she still hadn't been in, telling her that their dinner would have to be postponed. He had every intention of ringing her later although by now David would have explained what had happened.

Tossing his keys onto the hall table, he headed for the kitchen to make himself something to eat, sharply reminded by the growling of his empty stomach that he hadn't had time for lunch. He was just examining the less-than-inspiring contents of his fridge when the bell rang.

Sighing, Sam nudged the fridge door shut and went back down the hall, hoping that whoever it was wouldn't take too long. Impatiently he swung the front door open then felt his heart give an all too familiar lurch as he found Holly on the step.

'What are you doing here?' he asked in surprise. 'Didn't Mike give you my message?'

'Yes, and Dad told me what happened.' She held up a bulging carrier bag, laughing at his expression as he caught the appetising aroma wafting from it. 'I decided that if the doctor couldn't come to dinner than dinner had to come to the doctor! I seem to have arrived just in the nick of time, too. I'd say we have a severe case of hunger here, wouldn't you agree, Dr O'Neill?'

CHAPTER NINE

'THAT was absolutely delicious!' Sam sank back against the cushions with a sigh of contentment.

'I'm glad you enjoyed it.' Holly smiled as she gathered up their dirty plates. 'I wish I could claim the credit for cooking it, but that goes to Rose. I phoned the pub after Mike gave me your message and asked her if she could do something to take out. And *voilà*…chicken in lemon sauce! Beats beans on toast, which is the limit of my culinary expertise.'

He laughed. 'Well, whoever cooked it *you* were the one with the brilliant idea of bringing it round here. I really appreciate it, Holly. Thank you.'

'Don't mention it.' She gave him a wide smile, although her eyes held just a hint of uncertainty. 'You're sure you didn't mind, Sam? I wouldn't want you to think that I was pushing things too far.'

He reached out and brushed her cheek with a gentle finger. 'I don't think any such thing. It was a great idea.' He took a quick breath but the words had to be said. 'I was so disappointed when I thought our evening had to be cancelled.'

'So was I.' She didn't add anything more as she got up and carried their plates out to the kitchen. He rested his head against the cushions and closed his eyes, trying not to think about what he'd done. Whether it was wise or not, he refused to pretend that missing their date would have meant nothing to him.

He opened his eyes as he heard her coming back into the room, and quickly got up to move the coffee-table closer to the sofa so she could set the tray down on it.

'Black, two sugars?' she asked, picking up the cafetière and pouring coffee into one of the cups.

'Uh-huh.' Sam accepted the cup with a grin.

'What?' she asked, putting the pot down on the tray and frowning at him.

'Oh, I was just thinking that your stint in Reception—short though it was—has paid dividends. You know just how I like my coffee,' he teased.

She raised her eyes. 'Mmm, typical male—thinks only of his own comforts.' Picking up the pot once more, she poured herself a cup of coffee. 'Anyway, apart from it being a wonderful opportunity to learn how you like your coffee, I enjoyed working in the surgery. I was sorry when Liz told me that Eileen would be back today.'

'It was funny not seeing you there this morning. I missed you.' He took a gulp of coffee when he realised how revealing that had been. In the past, he'd always kept some distance between himself and the women he'd gone out with, but he found it increasingly difficult to do that with Holly—and his own vulnerability scared him a little.

He got up to switch on the stereo, avoiding looking at her as he sorted through the stack of CDs piled up on the shelf next to it. 'How about this?' he asked, choosing one at random.

'Fine.' She picked up a spoon and stirred her coffee. He adjusted the volume so that the music provided a gentle background. 'I missed being there and seeing you...all.'

She quickly tagged on the last word, as though afraid that she might have overstepped the boundaries. Sam realised how hard it was going to be to keep a check on every word they said and what a strain it would be as well. He put the CD case back on the shelf with a clatter which made her look up.

'Let's make a pact, Holly, that for what little time we have together we don't spoil it by always wondering if we're saying the wrong thing.'

'Sounds good to me.' She gave a light laugh. Curling her legs under her, she settled against the arm of the sofa as she sipped her coffee. 'This is a lovely song. I haven't heard it before—who's singing it?'

Sam grimaced. 'I've no idea.'

They both laughed and it broke the tension. After that it was much easier to relax again. They discussed what music they liked, which books they'd read and films they'd seen, finding to their astonishment that they had similar tastes.

Holly laughed as he ruefully admitted to a love of old musicals. 'You don't have to look so embarrassed. I adore those old spectaculars, no matter how corny the story lines are. At least you know there's going to be a happy ending and the handsome hero is going to get his girl.'

'So, a true romantic at heart, are you?' he teased, grinning at her and thinking how lovely she looked. He'd only switched on a couple of table lamps and their soft glow enhanced her delicate prettiness. She was wearing a simple white blouse and slim-fitting trousers in a muted green, her feet pushed into flat leather sandals. Her hair was softly waving around her face, the honey-brown curls glistening in the lamplight.

Sam thought that he'd never seen her looking more lovely than she looked right then, relaxed and smiling. He could just imagine how it would be to spend every evening like this, to look forward to coming home, knowing that she'd be there—

He felt his heart jolt as he pulled up short. He was letting his imagination run away with him again. It was one thing to agree to spend time together over the next few weeks and something else entirely to start thinking along those lines. It was a relief when the telephone suddenly rang because it gave him a much-needed excuse to get himself in hand. Soft lights and a beautiful woman weren't the best inducements to rational thought.

The call was from Lucy Fleming to say that Ben, her six-month-old son, was running a temperature. Sam took down the details and quickly assured her that he'd be there in a few minutes. He went back to the sitting-room and found Holly loading their coffee-cups onto the tray. 'I have to go out, I'm afraid.'

'Nothing serious, I hope?' she asked with a frown.

'I don't think so. Lucy Fleming's little boy has a temperature and she's worried about him. I'll just go and take a look.'

'Shall I stay here and wait till you get back? Or would you rather I left?' She stood up, the tray in her hands.

'No, don't go,' he found himself saying. He gave her a crooked grin, wondering if she suspected how much he wanted her to stay. 'Hopefully, it won't take long, and it seems a shame to spoil the evening.'

'Right. I…I'll just take these through to the

kitchen and wash them, then.' She gave him a quick smile as she left the room but he saw the sparkle of pleasure in her eyes which she was unable to hide. He sighed as he left the house, wondering if he should have cut short the evening after all. It wasn't just Holly's feelings he was toying with here but his own. Every minute he spent with her was going to make it that much harder for him when the time came to leave.

He was gone longer than he'd expected. Baby Ben had a chest infection and his temperature was high enough to keep Sam at the Flemings' house until he was sure the little boy was responding to treatment. A mild analgesic especially formulated for infants, plus sponging with tepid water, did the trick in the end. The course of antibiotics he prescribed should clear up the child's chest, although he told Lucy Fleming to ring him again if she was worried.

He let himself into the house, pausing in the hallway as silence greeted him. Holly must have decided to go home after all when he hadn't come back as promised, he realised with a pang of disappointment.

He glanced into the sitting-room but, as expected, there was no sign of her. He carried on to the kitchen and poured himself a glass of orange juice. The chicken had been delicious but it had left him feeling very thirsty. He took a deep swallow from the glass then glanced at his watch, surprised to see that it was gone ten o'clock already.

He finished the juice and wondered whether to watch television before going to bed, but the thought held little appeal. He went into the sitting-room to switch off the lamps and came to an abrupt halt as he discovered Holly curled up on the sofa fast asleep.

She had her cheek pillowed on her hand and her lips were slightly parted as she breathed softly. She looked so utterly adorable that he felt his heart contract as he was swamped by a whole host of emotions.

He wanted simply to stand there and just watch her sleeping, yet at the same time was sorely tempted to run his fingers down her velvet-soft cheek and wake her up…

'Sam?' She must have somehow sensed he was there because her eyes opened and he felt a spasm run through him as he saw the instant recognition they held. She struggled to sit up, running a hand through her hair to push it away from her face. 'I must have fallen asleep. What time is it?'

'Gone ten.'

'Ten! But you should have woken me,' she replied, looking flustered.

'I've only just got back,' he explained hurriedly. 'And I was just debating whether to wake you, only I couldn't decide if I should do it the tried and tested way or not,' he added in a deliberately teasing tone because he was still shaken by the depth of emotion he'd felt just now.

'The tried and tested way?'

She frowned as she looked up at him with sleepy emerald eyes and he only just managed not to groan. Had she no idea how delectable she looked at that moment, all soft and warm with sleep? Steadfastly, he kept all trace of what he was feeling out of his voice but it was an effort all the same.

'Don't tell me you never read any fairy stories when you were a little girl?'

She gave a wicked laugh. 'Oh, that way! I see.

The problem is that I'm not Sleeping Beauty and, unless I've got your profession wrong, you aren't Prince Charming either,' she retorted pithily.

'Well, I think that answers my question, doesn't it?'

He gave a rueful laugh which ended abruptly as Holly said softly, 'Does it?'

He would have had to be blind not to see the invitation in her eyes, and made from stone to ignore it. When she held her hand out to him he took it immediately and pulled her to her feet, but once she was standing there in front of him he found himself at a loss to know what to do. He, Sam O'Neill, suddenly had no idea what to do with this beautiful, sexy woman who was looking at him with such…such desire!

His hands rose then fell back to his sides like two lead weights. He saw the puzzlement that crossed her face and felt as bewildered as she obviously did. What on earth was the matter with him? Why was it so hard to do what his instincts were telling him to?

'Sam…what is it?'

Her voice was husky and he shivered as he felt it run along his rawly sensitive nerves. His mouth felt so parched again that he had to wet his lips. He saw her eyes follow the movement of his tongue…

His hands clenched as a spasm of desire hit him so hard that afterwards he wondered how he'd managed to stay upright. And yet still he found himself unable to make that first move. One step, the smallest dip of his head and their lips would touch… That was all it had taken so many times in the past. But this wasn't just any woman. This was Holly and that made a world of difference.

'Maybe this isn't how it happens in those fairy stories but women don't always need to be swept off their feet…'

It was Holly who took that one small step, her hands that reached out to draw his head down and her lips that made that first contact…

After that it was easy.

Sam felt the blood rush to his head as movement came back to him. His hands rose and gripped her shoulders, his fingers closing firmly around her soft flesh. He felt Holly smile against his mouth, heard her whisper something, but he couldn't hear what it was through the pounding of his heart. Then her mouth clung to his, allowing no more leeway for words.

He drew her closer until their bodies were locked together, her breasts pushing against the wall of his chest, her hips pressing against his so that there was no chance that she couldn't tell how much he wanted her. He didn't care. He wanted her so much that he ached in places he hadn't known existed before.

He framed her face with his hands as he deepened the kiss, felt the shuddering response she gave to the first delicate probing of his tongue as it explored the secret places of her mouth. He understood at once when she suddenly drew away because it *was* almost too much to bear.

'I never thought…never imagined…' She took a deep breath, her breasts pushing against his chest again as she dragged air into her lungs but his arms contracted convulsively and pushed it right out again.

'That it could be like this,' he finished for her, his voice filled with tender understanding.

'Yes.' She drew back to look at him and he saw

the question in her eyes even though he knew she'd never ask it.

He drew her head to his shoulder and kept it there, not wanting to look at her in case he said more than he could afford to say. No promises, no commitments. It was harder than ever to recall the familiar litany.

'Neither did I,' he admitted roughly, holding her even closer in the hope that it would quell the ache in his heart, but how could it do that? Holding her like this, it just made things worse because he was more aware than ever of what he would have to give up in a few weeks' time.

She must have sensed his thoughts somehow because her voice was tinged with pain. 'If only this could have happened some other time…'

'But it didn't. And we have to play the hand we've been dealt, Holly, or…or get out of the game.' His voice shook because he couldn't imagine what it would be like if she chose the latter.

'That isn't what I want, Sam. No matter what, I won't regret this.'

There was just enough conviction in her voice to convince him. He kissed her again with a hungry urgency that stopped any more questions. She wrapped her arms around his neck and held him, her fingers sliding into the crisp black hair at the back of his head. The kiss went on and on until they were both breathless, when they broke apart.

Sam ran the tip of his finger over her kiss-ripened mouth, his heart pounding so hard that it felt as if it would explode. He wanted to kiss her again and again—never stop—but he knew that if they didn't end this now then there'd be no going back. 'I think I'd better take you home, don't you?'

'Yes.' She made no protest as she slipped out of his arms and picked up the sweater she'd left draped over the arm of the sofa. Pulling it over her head, she shook her hair free and looked at him with steady green eyes. 'I've never slept with any man, Sam. I've never wanted to—until now. I just wanted you to know that.'

She turned and walked from the room but for a moment he didn't follow her. He couldn't, just as he couldn't begin to describe how he felt at that moment. He felt both ten feet tall and near despair. No woman had ever made him feel this way before, aching for her yet at the same time fiercely determined to safeguard her innocence.

He sighed as he followed her out to the hall. Another time, another place and it might have been so different.

The next few days flew past. Elizabeth's father was now off the critical list. His doctors were cautiously optimistic but there was no possibility of him making the long journey home just yet.

After much heart-searching it was decided to postpone the wedding until December when Charles Allen should be fit to fly home. Elizabeth would stay in Australia for another few weeks, which meant that they had to cope as best they could with one member of staff less.

Sam felt as though he was on some sort of crazy treadmill, running faster and faster just to stand still. He couldn't stop time slipping away and each morning he awoke to the thought that it was one day closer to him leaving.

He saw Holly several times—for a drink or a visit to the cinema—and each time they met it seemed as though they discovered something else new and fascinating about each other. It both delighted and scared him. The more he grew to know and like about her the more he had to lose.

There were just two weeks left to Sam's tenure in Yewdale when he was called to Yewthwaite Farm once again early one morning, this time to see old Mrs Walsh. However, there was little he could do. The old lady had died peacefully in her sleep, just short of her ninety-first birthday.

'If she had to go then at least it was here in her own bed.' Harvey wiped his eyes. 'And she weren't in any pain so that's a blessing.'

'It is. Your mother had a long and happy life, Harvey. And you and Helen should be proud of the way you looked after her,' Sam said gently, as he accompanied them down to the kitchen.

'She could be a bit of a stickler at times but I'll miss her. My mother died when I was just a child and Harvey's mum seemed to take her place.' Helen blew her nose. 'I was very fond of her.'

'As she was of you, Helen.' Sam turned to her, thinking how worn out she looked. Suddenly he made up his mind that in the short time left to him he was going to get to the bottom of Helen's problems somehow. 'The last time I came out here, Harvey's mother called me in to speak to her. She was worried about you.'

'About me?' Helen turned away abruptly and picked up the kettle. 'I can't think why.'

'Can't you?' he asked quietly, and Helen glanced at him. 'I'm not trying to press you into doing anything you don't want to. I'd just like to help if I can. Ring me any time you feel you want to, Helen.'

He left it at that, hoping that Helen would take what he'd said to heart. It would be nice to think that he'd resolved that problem when he left...

He sighed as he pulled out onto the main road. If only there was a solution to his own problems. But no matter how hard he tried he couldn't think of one.

'Oh, there you are, Sam. I was wondering where you'd got to.'

David appeared, looking decidedly harassed. Sam put down his pen and stretched. He'd spent his supposedly free afternoon catching up on paperwork and he was stiff from bending over the desk for so long.

'Problems?' he queried.

'Aren't there always?' David came into the room and closed the door. There was a baby clinic that afternoon, which James was taking, and the surgery was busy. 'I've just had Ian Farnsworth on the phone for starters. Evidently, the Merseyside police have contacted him because young Jason has gone missing again. They think he might be trying to make his way back here.'

'Not again!' Sam groaned.

'Afraid so. Anyway, Ian asked if we could keep an eye open for the boy so I'm passing the message along,' David explained. 'And I've just had a call from the suppliers, wanting to know when we intend to install the new computer system. I think they're tired of us dragging our heels.'

'It does seem to be taking a long time, doesn't it?' Sam agreed. The new computer system would be state of the art and would provide them with many extra facilities, the most important being a direct video link to the local hospital. Patients would be able to come into the surgery and speak to a consultant about a range of problems, thereby sparing them a fifty-mile round trip.

'It does. It's all down to money, of course. Until we're sure that we can find the finance then we simply cannot go ahead. But if we delay much longer we're going to lose this deal and it was the best one we had by far. I'll just have to see if I can stall them for another week or so.'

He paused, giving Sam the distinct impression that there was something else worrying him.

'Was there something else, David?' he prompted, although it wasn't like the older man to be reticent.

'Yes.' David sighed. 'Look, I know this is none of my business but I have to say something.'

Sam got up and went to the window. 'This is about Holly, isn't it?' he asked levelly.

'Yes. Oh, I know she's a grown woman but she's still my daughter and I care about her. You two have been seeing one another quite a lot recently and I don't want her getting hurt. She's been through enough in the past few years. I hope you'll bear that in mind, Sam.'

David didn't add anything more but, then, he didn't need to. Sam understood his concerns because they were the same ones he had. *He* didn't want

Holly to get hurt but there was no guarantee it wouldn't happen. Had he been wrong to let this situation develop?

'Penny for them, O'Neill.'

He glanced round, fixing a smile to his mouth as he saw Abbie. 'I don't think they're worth a penny. You can have them for free if you'd like.'

'Sounds very grim.' Abbie perched on the corner of the desk and regarded him thoughtfully. 'David was looking a bit uptight just now—should I be adding two and two and making five?'

'Is nothing private in this place?' Sam sighed, only half joking.

'Nope. You should know that by now, Sam. This town is a real hotbed of gossip.' The teasing note in her voice didn't manage to disguise her concern.

He sat down again, tipping his chair back as he stared at the ceiling. 'So what's on the gossip agenda at the moment? Or do I need to ask that?'

'Probably not.' Abbie sighed. 'It's common knowledge that you and Holly have been seeing one another. Do I take it that David isn't too happy about it?'

'He's worried that I might hurt Holly.'

'And will you?'

The question caught him off guard. The chair thudded back onto all four legs as he started to deny it. 'Of course not.' He stopped and sighed. 'I don't want to hurt her, believe me. I…I care too much about her. But with me going away it isn't easy to know what to do for the best.'

'Then maybe you should think really hard about what you want,' Abbie suggested quietly, the tiniest hint of sadness in her voice. 'Sometimes we get so set on a course that it seems impossible to make any changes. But if you care about her then you can find a way around this, Sam. It all depends on how important it is to you.'

She stood up with a self-conscious laugh. 'I'm wasted here. I should be writing for one of the glossies. I'd make the perfect agony aunt, especially as I'm so good at giving advice and so bad at taking it.'

Sam smiled, although his mind was whirling. Was Abbie right? Was there a way around this situation? It seemed impossible to him but maybe he wasn't trying hard enough to find a solution...

Did he really *want* to find one when it might mean changing all his plans? The trouble was that he wasn't sure what he wanted any more. 'Well, I'll bear in mind what you said, *Aunty* Abbie!'

'Good... Oh, I almost forgot what I came in for. We've decided to throw a leaving party for you, seeing that so many people keep asking what we're doing to mark the occasion. The vicar has offered to let us use the church hall so a week on Saturday seems like the best day. You leave the following Wednesday, don't you? I hope that's OK with you?'

'It's fine but I really wasn't expecting any fuss,' Sam said, touched by the offer.

'You didn't honestly imagine that we'd let you go without a proper send-off?' She shook her head. 'No way, O'Neill. You're getting the full works so be warned!'

She hurried off and Sam tried to apply himself to the paperwork once more, but his mind wasn't on it.

He kept wondering if Abbie had been right to suggest he find a compromise, but was it what he wanted? And was it what Holly wanted? Perhaps that was the most crucial question of all. How did she really feel about him? He both wanted to know and was afraid of the answer because, whatever it was, it was going to change his life.

hurried towards the front reception. 'I thought he had a doctor flat by now? Didn't you say that Mike finished work last week? Can't we contact him there?'

'Mike was on call this morning so Holly told me to ring for him here,' Laura said. 'I'll see what we can do.'

CHAPTER TEN

SAM had arranged to take Holly out for a meal that night so he picked her up just before seven. Several times he'd thought about what David had said to him and wondered if he was doing the right thing, but in the end he couldn't bring himself to cancel their date. Maybe it was selfish but he just wanted to be with her for the short time they had left.

She answered the door to him and he whistled appreciatively as he took stock of the chic raspberry-pink dress she was wearing that night. She'd pinned her hair into a French pleat, the fan of loose curls sprouting from the top of it adding a fun note to the elegant style. She looked so young and lovely as she stood in the doorway, smiling at him, that he felt his heart skip a beat with pure pleasure.

'You look lovely,' he said sincerely.

'Thank you, kind sir. One tries one's best, especially as this is a night for celebration,' she replied, laughing at him.

'Is it, indeed? And what exactly are we celebrating?' He raised his brows but she shook her head, making the silky fan of curls bob about.

'Oh, you'll have to wait till later to find that out,' she declared. She looked over her shoulder as Laura came along the hall. 'Tell Dad I'll see him later, will you, Laura? But you won't tell him my news, will you?'

'Of course not.' Laura smiled as she kissed the

younger woman's cheek affectionately. 'I have no intention of stealing your thunder.'

Holly laughed as she gave Laura a swift hug. 'Thanks.'

She quickly headed out to the car, leaving Sam wondering what was going on. It all sounded very mysterious but, true to her word, she made no attempt to explain as they drove to the restaurant near Newthwaite where he'd booked a table for them.

It was one of his favourite places to eat, although it was the first time Holly had been there. Three tiny stone cottages had been cleverly converted into a dining area and fitted out with old-fashioned tables and chairs. Sparkling white linen and soft lighting added to the ambience of the place. The restaurant had been open only six months but had quickly gained a reputation for its excellent cuisine so that it was full.

They were shown to a table by the window, which gave a wonderful view down the valley towards Yewdale Water. Holly sighed as she stared at the familiar landscape. 'No matter how often you see it, it's still one of the most stunning views in the world.'

'It is. I never tire of it myself. Thank you.' He accepted the menu from their waiter and opened it, glancing up as he became aware that Holly was watching him. 'What?'

'Oh, I was just thinking that if you like it here so much one day you might be tempted to come back.'

He set the menu beside his plate as he looked at her. 'It has crossed my mind recently.'

'Has it, Sam?' She glanced round as the waiter came to take their order. He'd obviously assumed that they were ready to order as neither of them were paying any attention to the menu.

Sam ordered from memory while Holly hurriedly looked at what was on offer, but after the waiter had gone again he would have been hard-pressed to say what he'd asked for. His heart was racing almost out of control as he wondered what he'd say if Holly pressed him further.

He'd told her the truth because he *had* thought about coming back to Yewdale, but it depended upon so many other factors—and the biggest one of all was Holly herself. How could he take that first difficult step towards making such a commitment unless he was sure how she really felt about him?

'Why, if it isn't Dr O'Neill.'

He looked up as he recognised the booming voice, not sure whether he felt pleased or sorry about the interruption. It had got him off the hook but was that what he really wanted? He chased away that thought as he stood up to shake Tom Roughley's hand. 'Hello, Mr Roughley. Fancy seeing you here of all places.'

'Oh, I like to get out and about, especially now that I'm mobile again,' Tom replied.

'I take it that your knee is better?' Sam asked, noticing that there was no sign of the heavy bandages now.

'Oh, it's fine. I still get the odd twinge but nothing to worry about,' Tom assured him airily. He turned to Holly. 'And who is this lovely young lady, then?'

'Oh, I'm sorry.' Sam quickly made the introductions and saw Tom frown as he shook Holly's hand.

'Ross, did you say? Not related to Dr David Ross by any chance?'

'Dr Ross is my father. Have you met him?' Holly replied with a smile.

'Not face to face but I've spoken to him a couple of times on the phone. In fact, that's why Mavis and I are back in the area.' He must have seen from their blank expressions that neither of them had any idea what he meant. 'We're interested in buying the house when it comes onto the market. Landlord at the pub told us that it might be coming up for sale. Mavis and I went home and talked abut it and decided that we liked this area so much we wanted to live here— so I gave your father a call.'

Tom broke off as a waiter came over to him. 'Ah, seems our dinner is ready. I'd better get back otherwise I'll never hear the last of it.'

He gave them a cheery wave as he hurried back to his table. Sam looked curiously at Holly, 'Did you know that David was thinking about selling the house?'

'He's mentioned it several times. Obviously, it doesn't make sense to keep two houses next door to each other.'

'So, how do you feel about the idea?' Sam asked softly, watching her face and hoping that she wouldn't be too upset.

She shrugged. 'It's strange to think of the house where I grew up being sold but I'm sure it's the right thing to do. Dad and Laura would be better off starting afresh.'

'You and Laura seem to be getting along all right from what I've seen. Does that mean that you've got used to the idea of her and David?'

'Yes. Oh, I didn't want to, I have to admit.' She laughed ruefully. 'After I got over the initial shock I made up my mind that I would just have to put up with the situation. But it's difficult *not* to like Laura, isn't it? She's genuinely kind and caring—it isn't just an act. Seeing how happy she and Dad are, and how much Mike and Emily love her, it helped me see sense. I'm really glad that things worked out how they did for them.'

'That's great. It must be a huge relief for David as well. I know he was worried about you accepting her,' Sam said quietly.

'I'm sure it is. I put Dad through a lot of heartache and I regret that, but at the time it was the only way I could cope. Anyway, I have bit of news which I'm sure he's going to be delighted about.' She took a deep breath then made the announcement. 'I'm going back to medical school, Sam.'

'Really? Oh, I'm so pleased for you.' He reached over and squeezed her hand. 'Is that why we should be celebrating tonight?'

'Uh-huh! Remember that night I brought dinner round to your place? Well, the reason you couldn't get hold of me was because I'd driven to Liverpool to speak to one of my course tutors. Laura arranged it for me—she knows him from way back and asked him if he would see me.'

'And he persuaded you?'

'Oh, no,' she denied hastily. 'We talked it all through, but he left it to me to make up my mind if it was what I really wanted.'

'And you're quite sure it is what you want, Holly?' he asked quietly, running his thumb over the back of her hand.

'Yes.' The look she gave him was full of assurance. 'It's funny because I've felt as though I couldn't make up my mind about anything since Mum died, but suddenly I know exactly what I want to do—go back to complete my studies. It's the right thing for me.'

And after that? Sam wanted to ask. After she'd qualified, then what? Had she thought that far ahead, made plans? Did *he* feature in them? Did he want to?

The questions clamoured for answers but he wasn't sure even now if he had the right to ask them. Until he knew what *he* wanted, he couldn't ask anything of her.

The waiter arrived with their first course at that moment. Sam was glad when the conversation moved along more general channels because he felt so mixed up. One side of him wanted to promise Holly the world while the other—conditioned over the years—shied away from doing any such thing.

Despite everything, he enjoyed the evening. How could he not? He and Holly were simply on the same wavelength, laughing at the same jokes, interested in the same things. Before they knew it, it was time to leave. He took her hand as they walked across the car park. There were steps leading to the terraced gardens close to where they'd parked, and when she suggested they go there to look at the view one last time he agreed at once.

There was a chill in the air as it swept up from the valley and he felt her shiver as the breeze touched her bare arms.

'Here, put this on. You're going to catch cold.' He quickly shrugged off his jacket and draped it around her shoulders.

'But you'll be cold now,' she protested, trying to give it back to him.

He turned her round to face the view, drawing her

back against him as his arms slid around her waist.
'I'll let you keep me warm instead.'

'Sounds fair enough.' There was a husky note in
her voice which sent a frisson down his spine. He
bent and brushed a kiss against the side of her neck
and heard her murmur as she snuggled closer.
Involuntarily, his arms tightened and he felt his body
stir in immediate response to her closeness.

He loosened his hold just a little, breathing in her
delicate scent as he looked towards the silvery shim-
mer of the water in the distance. It was a moment
which he knew was going to stay with him for ever
because it was the moment he realised how much he
loved her.

He must have made some small sound as the
thought slid home because she turned her head to
look at him. 'Sam, what is it?'

He shook his head because he simply couldn't answer that question with anything less than the truth,
and the truth scared him. His lips brushed her cheek
and he saw her smile as she turned that last little bit
so that their mouths met.

Her lips were cool from the breeze yet beneath the
chill there was a fire that heated his blood as though
someone had put a match to dry tinder. Sam felt a
hot rush of desire race through him and he groaned.
It took only a split second to turn her into his arms
but even that was too long when every cell in his
body was aching for the feel of her.

His lips were urgent as they merged with hers yet
she met their demand with an eagerness that simply
increased his need of her. He couldn't seem to get
enough of her mouth, drink in sufficient of her sweet-

ness, hold her close enough to fill the emptiness of his arms…

His hands slid beneath the folds of the jacket and followed the soft curves of her body, moving so delicately over her breasts that his fingers barely brushed them yet he felt the way her nipples hardened immediately beneath his fingertips.

His breath caught on a wave of desire so fierce and so strong that he trembled. She felt it at once. Her hands came up to smooth his back, her palms running softly over the taut muscles beneath his thin cotton shirt. He trembled again, and felt the shiver that ran through her.

'Sam.'

His name was all the invitation he needed as he bent to kiss her again…

'Night, Dr O'Neill. Oh, and you, too, Miss Ross!'

Tom Roughley's cheery farewell broke the spell abruptly. Sam took a deep breath as he let Holly go but he could feel himself trembling with the aftermath of their passion.

'Honestly, Tom. Trust you…' Mavis Roughley was still berating her husband for his lack of tact as she hustled him towards their car. Holly laughed wryly as she watched them drive away, still squabbling.

'Oh, dear, I think we're the cause of that row, don't you?'

'Looks like it, although the Roughleys don't need much excuse from what I've seen so far.' Sam managed a laugh but he could hear the strain it held. 'We'd better get back as well.'

'I suppose you're right.' She led the way up the steps to the car. They said little on the drive back to

Yewdale. Both of them seemed to have a lot on their minds—Sam knew he did! He slowed as they came to the turning to Holly's house.

'I don't want to go home yet, Sam.'

He looked at her in surprise, feeling his heart begin to drum as he saw the expression in her eyes. He knew what she was saying but he still had to ask the question to be sure. 'Then where do you want to go?'

'To your house…to stay the night. But only if it's what you want as well, Sam.'

Of course it was what he wanted! He couldn't think of anything he'd wanted so much in the whole of his life. And yet he knew in his heart that he couldn't let it happen.

'I…I don't think that would be a good idea.' His voice grated from the sheer effort of forcing the words out. He saw her face close up and the hurt that shimmered in her eyes before she looked away and reached for the doorhandle.

'I understand. I'm sorry if I embarrassed you—'

'No!' he caught hold of her arm and stopped her as she tried to get out of the car. 'It isn't that at all.'

'Then what is it? Tell me, Sam.' She gave a broken laugh. 'I can't claim to be an expert in this area but I got the impression that you wanted to make love to me.'

'I did…I do!' He took her face between his hands and made her look at him so that she could see he was telling the truth. 'But it wouldn't be right, Holly.'

'Why not, if it's what both of us want?'

'Because you might come to regret it. You told me that you haven't slept with anyone before—there must be a reason for that.'

'There is. I told you that as well. I've never met anyone I wanted to make love with until I met you.'

There was no doubt that she was telling the truth. He had to steel himself to go on. 'I'm flattered, Holly—'

'Flattered?' She stared at him with eyes that were starting to show the first glimmer of anger. 'Is that all it means to you, Sam—a boost to your ego?'

'No, of course not!' He felt his own temper stir. This was the hardest thing he'd ever had to do and she wasn't making it easy for him. 'I'm just saying that it needs some thought—'

'Maybe you can be so clinical about your emotions but I can't!' Once again she cut him off, her eyes sparkling. 'I'm beginning to see what a fool I've been. I should have realised that someone with your reputation has to be able to…to remain detached. And in all fairness you have tried to warn me that you weren't looking for a relationship. You never have been. That's why you've run through a stream of girlfriends in the time you've been here. *I* am just one of a very long list!'

She thrust open the car door and got out. He wanted to tell her to stop, to make her believe that she was wrong, but the words wouldn't come. In his heart he knew that the one sure way to convince her was to tell her the truth—that he loved her and that there would never be another woman he would feel like this about. What held him back was his fear that revealing his true feelings would leave himself open to hurt.

Holly had admitted she was attracted to him—he didn't need any proof of that—but did she love him?

It was funny to think that his whole future was hanging in the balance because of just three little words…

Sam was rostered for surgery on the morning of his farewell party. He was glad. The less time he had to brood about what had happened the better.

He hadn't seen or spoken to Holly since she'd got out of the car that night. He knew it was up to him to try to clear up the misunderstanding but something held him back.

He had a contract to fulfil and Holly had her studies—there was no future for them when they'd be thousands of miles apart in a few days' time. Better accept that and get on with his life. But no matter how sensible it all sounded it didn't make it any easier to accept the situation.

Few people turned up for surgery that morning, which wasn't unusual as only urgent cases were seen on Saturdays. He sent Eileen home early when it looked as though nobody else was going to arrive. He was just switching the phones through to the on-call setting when Helen Walsh came in.

'Oh, I'm sorry. I should have come earlier…' She made as though to leave but there was no way that Sam was letting her go now that she'd got this far.

'Come in, Helen,' he said firmly, leading the way to his consulting-room and giving her little option but to follow him. She hesitated just inside the doorway, looking nervous and ill at ease.

'Come and sit down, Helen,' he urged gently. 'I'm glad you've decided to come. I was hoping you would.'

'I've been trying to pluck up courage ever since you came to the farm when Harvey's mum died,' she admitted in a low voice as she finally sat down on the chair.

'And now you have. That's the first step and it's always the most difficult.' He carried on when she still couldn't bring herself to speak about her problems. 'Maybe it would help if I told you what Mrs Walsh said to me that day I spoke to her. She told me that your mother had been very ill when you were a little girl and that your father couldn't deal with the situation and left home.'

'Yes.' Tears suddenly spilled from Helen's eyes. 'It was awful. Mum was so ill and he just upped and went—'

'And you were afraid that the same thing could happen to you?' Sam suggested gently as she broke off.

'I keep thinking about Dad and how he couldn't cope with Mum being ill, then wondering how Harvey would react.' Helen dabbed her eyes with a tissue. 'We don't even have any children. We always wanted a family but it just hasn't happened. Why would he want to stay with me if I ended up like my mother?'

'I think you're jumping the gun there, Helen. I know how devoted Harvey is to you. It's obvious how worried he's been about you recently.' Sam smiled encouragingly. 'The only thing Harvey wants is to see you well again so let's try to find out what is wrong, shall we?'

'Yes.' Helen squared her shoulders. 'I think it's about time I faced up to this, Dr O'Neill, and stopped pretending.'

'Good. Let's go right back to when you first began

feeling ill. Tell me what happened.' Sam picked up a pen ready to make notes.

'It all started around Christmas last year. I kept getting this tingling sensation in my legs, like pins and needles, but it went away after a week or so and I thought no more about it.'

'But it came back?' he prompted.

'Not so much a tingling but more a numbness this time. My legs seemed to feel heavy, almost as though they wouldn't hold me up.' She looked down at the tissue she was twisting nervously. 'When I fell down the stairs and sprained my ankle that time it was because they suddenly gave way, but I just pretended I'd slipped.'

'I see. And do I assume that's what happened when you had those other accidents?' he asked, frowning slightly.

'Not when I burnt my arm. I seem to get dizzy a lot at the moment. It comes on right out of the blue— one minute I'm fine and then the next the room starts to spin. That's how I fell onto the hot plate on the stove,' she confessed.

'I noticed that there was some visual disturbance as well when I examined you. Does that happen often?' he asked levelly, to put her at ease.

'Not really. It's only happened that one time. It really scared me because my mum lost her sight because of the brain tumour. Do...do you think that's what is wrong with me, Dr O'Neill?'

'Just because your mother had a brain tumour, it doesn't increase the chances of you having one, Helen,' he replied firmly. 'I think we should go with what we have and not speculate at this stage. I want to run some tests—blood, urine, that sort of thing for starters. And I also want to send you to hospital for a more in-depth investigation. MRI, or magnetic resonance imaging, can show up any abnormalities in the soft tissue in the brain.'

'I see. Well, I suppose it's better to know what you're dealing with.' Helen gave him a thin smile. 'Even though it's taken me long enough to realize it.'

'You've done the right thing, Helen. Trying to pretend everything was fine, it must have been a strain,' Sam said sympathetically as he got ready to take the blood sample.

'It was. It's a wonder Harvey hasn't packed his bags already after what I've put him through!' Helen joked but he could hear the worry in her voice.

'It'll be fine. You just tell Harvey the truth.' He didn't try to press her, realising that it was extremely difficult for her to admit her fears. He collected the samples and packed them up to send them off to the lab immediately.

Helen looked a little better when she got up to go. She seemed relieved to have got the whole story out into the open at last. 'Thank you, Dr O'Neill, both for your patience and for going to all this trouble for me. It's a shame you're leaving. The whole town is going to miss you.'

'And I'm going to miss being here,' he admitted. 'I've grown very fond of this place and everyone in it.'

'Then maybe you'll come back one day and make your home here.' Helen smiled warmly at him. 'You should think about it.'

Sam locked up after Helen left, thinking about what she'd said. Holly had said the same thing, that

he should think about returning to Yewdale to settle
down—but that had been before the row they'd had
the other night. He doubted if she cared one way or
the other now where he lived.

The church hall was packed when he arrived that
night. Someone had painted a banner in bright orange
letters and pinned it over the door. It read, 'Good
Luck, Dr O'Neill.' Everyone seemed to want to offer
their best wishes so that it took him ages to make
his way across the room to where his colleagues were
waiting for him.

'I never expected anything like this,' he said
wryly, accepting the drink Abbie thrust into his hand.

She laughed. 'I told you we'd give you a good
send-off, didn't I?'

'You did.' He took a sip of beer and smiled around
at the rest of the group, his eyes lingering hungrily
on Holly for a moment before he looked away as she
gave him a cool nod.

'James not arrived yet?' he asked in a falsely
cheerful tone. Seeing Holly again, being this close to
her... It was almost more than he could bear when
it was obvious that she hadn't forgiven him for what
had happened. Suddenly he knew that he had to find
a way to explain how wrong she'd been, whether it
was sensible or not.

'He should be here very soon—' Abbie broke off.
'Talk of the devil!'

Sam glanced round, gasping in surprise as he saw
both James *and* Elizabeth coming towards him.
'What are you doing here?'

'I couldn't miss your leaving do, could I?' she
replied with a laugh. 'I managed to get on an earlier

flight and flew into Manchester, where James picked me up. Father is so much better that there didn't seem any reason for me to stay any longer when there's so much to do here. I warn you, though, that I probably won't stay the course. That flight is a killer.'

'Well, I'm glad to see you no matter how long you stay,' Sam said sincerely, moving aside as Laura started asking Elizabeth about her journey. Someone jogged his elbow and he grimaced as beer slopped over the side of his glass and splattered Holly's skirt.

'Sorry,' he apologised, offering her his handkerchief to mop up the drops.

'That's OK.' She dabbed at the wet spots then gave the handkerchief back to him. 'So, are you all ready for Wednesday, then? Everything packed?'

'Not really. There's still loads to do but I expect it will all come right at the end of the day.' He sounded as stilted as she did, and he was suddenly irritated with the whole situation. 'Look, Holly, about the other night—'

'I don't want to discuss it, Sam. There doesn't seem much point.' She gave him a thin smile then went over to speak to Cathy Fielding, who was helping to set up the buffet in the far corner of the room and trying to stop a couple of children from filching any of the food.

Sam was tempted to go after her and make her listen to what he had to say, but how could he if she was determined not to? He summoned a smile as Abbie tapped him on the shoulder.

'How about a dance, Dr O'Neill?'

'Sure. Why not?' He put his glass down and followed her onto the floor, frowning as he glanced over to where the music was coming from. 'Is that young Mike in charge of the disco?'

'Mike and Danny Shepherd. Evidently the pair of them have done quite a few discos at various friends' parties. However, I warned them to bear in mind the average age of the people here and not to go too wild with the music.' Abbie laughed. 'The last thing we need is anyone having a heart attack tonight. We're not trying to drum up business!'

'Too right,' Sam agreed ruefully. They carried on dancing when the next record came on, a slow one this time. He held Abbie lightly in his arms as she chatted away about various things. His gaze skimmed around the room, although he refused to admit to himself whom he was looking for...

His eyes met Holly's across the room and he felt his heart contract on a spasm of pain as she deliberately looked away.

'You two need your heads knocked together!'

'Sorry?' He glanced at Abbie in surprise and heard her sigh.

'You and Holly. It's obvious that you've had some sort of disagreement. For heaven's sake, Sam, do something before it's too late.'

'It isn't that simple,' he said tightly.

'No?' She caught hold of his hand and quickly steered him between the other couples. Before he realised what was happening she'd stopped in front of Holly. 'This is your dance, I believe.'

She had gone before either of them could say a word. Sam took a deep breath but his heart was banging against his ribs with nerves. 'Would you like to dance?' he asked huskily.

'Are you sure you want me to?' she countered, looking straight at him.

'Quite sure.' He held out his hand and could have jumped for joy when she slid hers into it after only the tiniest hesitation. He drew her into his arms once they were on the floor and held her as close as propriety allowed, which wasn't close enough. It was almost unbearable, feeling her body brushing against his so seductively and not being able to do anything about it. It was a relief when the music changed to a pulsing disco beat so that he could lead her from the floor and end the torment.

'Too fast for me, I'm afraid. I prefer the slow ones,' he said with an attempt at lightness which didn't quite work.

'Me, too...so long as I'm dancing with the right person.'

His heart began to drum even harder as he heard the note in her voice. It took all his courage to ask the question but he had to know what the answer was. 'And am I that person, Holly?'

CHAPTER ELEVEN

HOLLY laughed softly but Sam could hear the uncertainty in her voice. 'I thought I'd made it clear how I felt the other night, Sam.'

'I— You— Oh, hell, we can't talk here.'

He grabbed hold of her hand and quickly steered her towards the door. He was aware that people were turning to stare at them but he couldn't care less at that moment what anyone thought. He was reaching for the doorhandle when a sudden loud explosion made the whole place shake.

'What the devil was that?' Sam was first out of the door but other people weren't far behind him as he ran down the path. A red glow lit up the sky and seemed to be coming from a building further along the road.

'Isn't that the pottery?' Holly said in horror.

'Looks like it.' He looked round as David joined them. 'Looks as though something has happened at the pottery.'

'I'll ring the emergency services,' David said tautly, taking his phone out of his pocket.

'We'd better get over there,' Sam said, glancing at the others. Most people had the same idea so that a small crowd soon gathered outside the burning building. Flames were shooting out of one of the ground-floor windows and the heat could be felt even from a distance.

'There's nobody in there, I hope,' he said grimly.

'Normally there wouldn't be, but Frank and some of the lads were going to load up the vans tonight as we've got a special order going out first thing in the morning.' It was Cyril Rogerson who answered. He'd worked at the pottery for years and his face was grim as he checked his watch. 'They should have finished by now with a bit of luck…'

He stopped as young Sean Jackson pushed his way through the crowd. 'Jason and Benny are in there!' he cried frantically, pointing towards the factory.

'What did you say?' Cyril grasped the boy by his shoulders and shook him.

'Benny Ryan is in there. He took some food from the party to Jason—you know, that lad who was staying at the Outward Bound centre. He's been hiding in there so the police wouldn't find him.'

'Are you sure?' Cyril demanded. 'If you're making this up…'

'I'm not.' Sean started to cry. 'Cross my heart and hope to die.'

'Is there a way into the building, avoiding the fire?' Sam asked, his heart turning over at the thought of anyone being trapped inside.

'Through the delivery bay round the back. The doors will be locked if Frank has finished but I've got a key here,' Cyril replied at once, pulling it from his pocket. 'But you can't go in there, Dr O'Neill. The whole place could go up at any minute. Wait till the fire brigade gets here.'

'It could be too late by then,' he grated, taking the key.

'Sam's right,' James put in grimly. 'We daren't risk waiting. We have to try and get them out of there before the whole building goes up.'

Cyril was obviously convinced now of the need for action. 'Then the best bet is through the loading bay. The fire is coming from the kilns. That part of the building has fire containment doors but they could have been damaged by the explosion.'

'Then there isn't any time to waste.' Sam looked at James. 'Ready?'

'As much as I'll ever be.'

'I'll come with you,' David put in immediately, but Sam shook his head.

'We don't want too many people wandering around inside there. If you and Liz could stay outside then we can bring any casualties out to you. Maybe Abbie could go back to the surgery and fetch some supplies. Bandages, saline—that sort of thing.'

'I'll run her back there—I've got my car,' Cyril offered at once. The crowd parted to let them through. Most people were looking dazed by what was happening, although several of the men had organised themselves into a firefighting team. There was a heavy-duty hose by the pottery's gatehouse and they'd linked it up to the water main.

'Please be careful, Sam!' Holly caught hold of his arm as he turned to hurry off, her eyes pleading.

He dropped a kiss on her upturned face then gently loosened her fingers. 'I shall. I've too much to lose by being anything else.'

He gave her a smile which said everything he couldn't at that moment, then he turned and ran towards the building with James close behind. The heat was intense until they reached the side away from the fire. The loading-bay doors were standing open and his heart plummeted.

'Looks as though Frank Shepherd must be still inside,' James observed grimly.

'Looks like it. We'd better get in there and see what's happened to him. And heaven alone knows where Jason and Benny will be,' Sam replied, sending up a prayer that they'd been well away from the explosion. He and James ran into the building through the loading bay but there was no sign of anyone.

'Where do you think they'll be?' James asked, looking at the crates of china stacked up to the ceiling.

'I've no idea,' Sam responded grimly, leading the way through heavy swing doors which gave access to the main part of the building. He could smell smoke and hear the fire roaring away but it hadn't reached this part of the building yet.

'Hello, can you hear me?' He cupped his hands round his mouth as he shouted, and thought he heard a faint cry from further along the corridor. He and James ran towards it and found Frank Shepherd huddled against the wall. His face was waxen and trickles of blood were running from both his ears.

'It's OK, Frank, just take it easy now.' Sam knelt down beside him. 'Can you tell me where you're hurt?'

'My chest… Can't seem to breathe. And my ears…' Frank groaned, closing his eyes as the effort of speaking proved too much for him.

'Right, don't try to say anything else. We'll soon have you out of here,' Sam assured him, glancing at James who was methodically checking Frank's injuries.

'Chest has been crushed by the blast. Obviously

multiple fractures. Look at the way it's moving when he breathes.'

'The danger is that his lungs will be damaged if they get pierced by one of those broken ribs,' Sam said worriedly as he saw how the chest wall was being sucked inwards with each breath instead of being pushed out. 'Also there's obviously damage to his eardrums. We'll have to get him out of here as fast as we can but he can't walk in that condition.'

'I'll go and fetch a couple of the men. There should be something lying around we can carry him on.' James hurried off to get help while Sam tried to make Frank comfortable. The man opened his eyes and made a supreme effort to speak.

'Two lads… Have to find them…'

'I will,' he assured him, looking round as he heard footsteps. 'How about the rest of your men, Frank? Are they still in here?'

'Went home… Spotted the lads and came back to find them… Went upstairs…' Frank's voice died away.

Sam stood up. 'I'm going upstairs to look for Jason and Benny,' he informed James as he arrived with a couple of men who were carrying a section of board to use as a makeshift stretcher.

'Be careful.' James's face was grim as he looked along the corridor where smoke was drifting about. 'The fire seems to be spreading fast now.'

'I will.' Sam didn't waste any more time as he ran to the stairs. The first floor contained offices and the staffroom, and he found Benny Ryan there, huddled in a corner with his arms over his head.

'Benny, it's me, Dr O'Neill. Are you hurt?'

'I's scared, Dr O'Neill,' Benny gave a gulping sob.

There was a long gash on his forehead which was oozing blood and another on his arm, but there didn't seem to be anything else wrong with him as far as Sam could tell. 'There was this big bang, see, and the windows all broke and the glass cut me—'

'It's OK, Benny.' Sam patted his shoulder. 'Don't be scared. We're going to get you out of here. Do you know where Jason is?'

'Dunno. Said as 'e was going to get a magazine from one of them offices, then there was this big bang and I hid in the corner,' he explained, his voice quavering.

'Well, don't you worry. We'll find him. Come on now.' Sam stood up but Benny shook his head as he cowered against the wall.

'There'll be more bangs. I want to stay here.'

'You can't. The building is on fire and we have to get you and Jason out,' Sam explained gently, trying desperately to reassure him. Although Benny had the mind of a child, he was a fully grown man and it would be impossible to manhandle him from the building. 'Come on now, Benny. Jason is your friend, isn't he? Don't you want to help me find him?'

'Well…' Benny hesitated then slowly struggled to his feet. He shambled along behind Sam as they made their way along the corridor, checking each of the offices in turn. There was quite a bit of damage— shattered windows, loosened sections of the ceiling, and so on. Jason was in the fifth office along, his left leg pinned under a filing cabinet which must have overturned when the explosion occurred.

'It's OK, son, we'll soon have you out of here.' With Benny's help Sam shifted the cabinet off the boy. He quickly checked Jason's leg and wasn't surprised to find the tibia was broken. There was a stack of old magazines by the desk and he quickly rolled several of them up to form a makeshift splint, using his belt and a scarf Benny found on a peg by the door to secure it in place.

'Right, I want you to be very brave now, Jason. That leg might hurt a bit but we have to get you out of here. OK?'

'OK.' Jason managed a grin as he ran a grimy hand over his face to wipe away the tears. 'This'll be something to tell my mates, won't it? It's like a story out of that series on the telly.'

Sam laughed ruefully. 'I suppose so.'

Carrying Jason as carefully as he could, he led the way back to the stairs, but when they got there he could see flames at the bottom. 'We'll have to find another way out,' he said levelly, not wanting to alarm Benny or Jason.

'There's a fire exit on the next floor. I've been using it to get in and out,' Jason put in quickly.

'Right. We'll give it a go.'

They made their way up the next flight of stairs but Sam's eyes were stinging from the smoke which was being funnelled up the stairwell. By the time they reached the fire exit all of them were coughing. Propping Jason against the wall, he pressed the release bar but the door wouldn't budge.

'It can't be locked!' Jason gasped in another lungful of air. 'I came in that way before. I've been leaving it wedged open so I can get in and out without anyone seeing me.'

'It must be jammed, then. Maybe the explosion caused some damage,' Sam said grimly, putting his shoulder to the door, but it still wouldn't open. 'We need something to lever it open with…'

He looked around, trying his best to contain his fear. If they couldn't get the door open, they were trapped. The fire had reached the floor below now and it would be only minutes before it moved upwards to where they were.

'There's some tools in that cupboard back there.' Jason pointed. He grinned sheepishly. 'I had a look round, you see, when there was nobody here.'

'I bet you did.' Sam ran to the cupboard, thanking heaven for the boy's inquisitiveness when he discovered several screwdrivers and a heavy hammer inside it. A couple of sharp blows with the hammer did the trick and the door sprang open at last.

Some of the bystanders must have heard the commotion because there were plenty of willing hands to take Jason from Sam as he stepped out onto the fire-escape platform. Benny had just started hurrying down the steps when there was another loud explosion which made the whole building shake.

Sam wasn't sure what happened then but something hit him on the side of the head. Blackness descended as though all the lights had suddenly gone out.

He spent the night in hospital. The section of iron guttering which had hit him had fractured his clavicle and given him a mild concussion so he wasn't allowed to sleep. He lay propped against a mound of pillows as the hours passed. It was the perfect opportunity to think, although he would have preferred a less draconian inducement!

As he lay there thinking back to that moment when

the world had gone dark he recalled his last thought—Holly. It had been her face that had followed him down into the darkness, hers he'd seen first when he'd awoken. She'd been kneeling beside him and the expression in her eyes at that moment was something that would stay with him until the day he died. It had certainly crystallised his thoughts!

He knew now exactly what he was going to do and it was a relief after all the uncertainty and heartache. He could hardly wait to see her again but he didn't expect her to appear as soon as she did. It was barely eight when she quietly slipped into the room.

'The nurse said that I could pop in as long as I promised not to excite you too much.'

'Did she, indeed?' He grinned wickedly as he held out his hand. 'I don't think there's much chance of you keeping to that, though!'

She chuckled as she took his hand and bent to kiss him, murmuring a protest as his lips clung to hers. 'You'll get me into trouble, Sam.'

'Would I do that?' He sighed as he patted the side of the bed. 'All right, I promise to be good so you're safe to sit down. What are you doing here so early, anyway?'

'I didn't go home.' She gently brushed his hair back from his forehead then let her hand rest against his cheek. 'I wanted to be here in case you needed me, Sam.'

'Darling, don't you know that I'll always need you?' He turned his head and kissed her palm, unable to contain his joy at hearing her words.

'Will you?' She took a deep breath and it seemed to him that she was steeling herself against the hurt which might follow. 'Are you sure, though, Sam? Really sure?'

'Yes!' He reached up to draw her down to meet his seeking lips then groaned as pain shot through him. 'Of all the times for this to happen.' He smiled as she laughed. 'Wicked woman—laugh at an injured man, would you?'

He sobered as he took hold of her hand again. 'I may not be able to prove I mean what I say but I hope you'll believe me anyway. I love you, Holly.'

'And I love you too, Sam, so much.' She bent towards him without any prompting and her lips were as eager as his as they kissed. Drawing back, she looked deep into his eyes. 'What made you finally realise how you felt?'

He stroked her cheek with a fingertip, glorying in the feel of her soft skin. 'That night on the terrace at the restaurant. I held you in my arms and suddenly I knew how much I loved you.'

'Then why did you refuse to take me back home with you? I don't understand.'

He smoothed away the frown lines from between her brows, his expression wry. 'Because I was being very noble and self-sacrificing. I wanted to make love to you, believe me. But it didn't seem the right thing to do when I'd be going away and couldn't offer you the commitment you deserved. I care about you too much to ever want to hurt you, darling.'

'Oh, Sam, you idiot! Why didn't you explain that to me? I would have understood and loved you all the more for it. Although I have to say that being noble doesn't suit you. I much prefer you as you are.' She brushed his mouth with a butterfly-soft kiss, laughing as he groaned when she moved out of reach.

'You deserve to suffer just a little for what you put me through.'

'Hard-hearted woman. Have you no compassion? Fine doctor you're going to make.'

'If I have to deal with patients like you then undoubtedly,' she retorted, then gasped as he tugged her down so that she landed next to him on the pillows. She could easily have escaped because with only one good arm he was somewhat hampered, but he was delighted when she didn't offer more than token resistance.

He looked into her sparkling eyes and his own were full of the wonderment of knowing how much she loved him. 'I never imagined it could feel like this.'

'To love and be loved?' She understood him so well that he felt choked with emotion. Burying his face in her hair, he nodded.

'I don't think you've had much experience of being loved, Sam. That's why you found it so difficult to accept what was happening.'

He nodded again. 'Yes. You're right, of course. I taught myself to keep people at a distance from an early age because I was afraid of getting hurt. It's probably the reason I've avoided any permanency in my life and all forms of commitment. It seemed safer that way.

'And then you came along and I found myself breaking every one of my own rules. I realised that I was getting involved despite myself and it scared me because I wasn't sure I could give you what you needed so much.'

'You mean stability and things like that?' She sighed. 'I can understand why you felt like that because I hadn't done a good job of handling Mum's death. Then there was the way I reacted when I first found out about Dad and Laura. I suppose I gave the impression of being, well, vulnerable.'

'That was it exactly. I could never have lived with myself if I hurt you as well, Holly.'

'But you aren't going to hurt me, Sam—not unless you tell me that you don't want me in your life any more.' Her voice broke. 'I don't think I could bear that.'

'You won't have to because it isn't going to happen.' He kissed her long and hard. 'We're going to find a way around this problem of us being separated!'

'Oh, Sam!'

He kissed her again, a kiss which promised to go on for some time but was interrupted when a nurse came into the room and cleared her throat. 'I think it's time you left, Miss Ross. Dr O'Neill needs his rest.'

Sam grinned, not at all abashed. 'There are a lot of things Dr O'Neill needs, but rest isn't one of them, Nurse.'

The middle-aged woman laughed. 'Well, they'll have to wait until you're discharged. If the doctor says it's all right, you should be leaving us by lunchtime. Think you can hang on till then?'

He caught hold of Holly's hand and kissed it. 'Just!'

He got up and dressed as soon as the doctor said that he could go. Holly had gone home to change after promising to come back for him later. It took a bit of persuasion—and a good deal of charm—but in the end the nurse agreed to let him visit Frank and Jason, who were in separate wards on the floor below.

Frank's wife, Jeannie, was sitting beside his bed and she smiled as she saw Sam. 'Hello, Dr O'Neill. How are you?'

'Not too bad. Once this collar-bone has healed I'll be fine. How are you feeling, Frank?'

'As though I've been run over by a ten-ton truck,' Frank retorted. 'Although from the look of all these bandages I could double as an Egyptian mummy.'

Sam grinned as he sat down on a hard hospital chair. 'Makes mine look very paltry in comparison. What did the doctor say?'

'Much as you'd expect—multiple fractures of the chest wall, burst eardrums,' Jeannie explained. 'Doctor said that Frank was lucky because if he hadn't had such prompt treatment it could have been a lot worse. That's all down to you and Dr Sinclair. We're really grateful.'

'Just doing our job.' Sam shrugged off her thanks but Frank wasn't letting it go at that.

'I'd call it more than that. You and Dr Sinclair did one heck of a job getting everyone out of there last night, and folk around her will remember that.'

'Well, as long as it all came right at the end of the day.' He got up to leave, a little embarrassed by the praise. 'I'm going to see how young Jason's doing now. Take it easy, Frank.'

Jason was sitting up in bed, looking extremely perky considering what he'd been through. He grinned when he saw Sam, pointing to the plaster that encased his leg. 'How about that, then? It's boss, isn't it?'

'Boss?' Sam's brows rose. 'Do I take that to mean you're pleased with your cast?'

'Course! What planet are you from?' Jason sighed heavily. 'Old folks always need everything explained to them.'

'Old! Cheeky monkey. Obviously I don't need to ask how you are, Jason. Last night's little escapade hasn't done much lasting damage.'

'I've got a broken leg!' Jason retorted, missing the point. 'Doctor says it'll be in plaster for weeks.'

'Then there won't be much chance of you getting up to any more mischief, will there? When are your parents coming to see you?'

'They're not.' Jason replied with feigned indifference. 'My mum went off a couple of years ago and I've never seen my dad. I live in a children's home.'

'Then maybe I can pop in and see you again while you're here?' Sam offered immediately, his heart aching for the boy because he, more than anyone, understood his situation.

'Up to you. I s'pose they'll make me go back soon, though.'

'Why did you run away? And why did you come back to Yewdale?' Sam asked curiously.

'Dunno. It was something to do, wasn't it? An adventure, like. And it's all right here, all sort of green and clean,' Jason muttered, as though ashamed of the admission.

'It's a nice place all right,' Sam replied softly, thinking to himself that he'd never uttered a truer statement. 'A good place to live.'

A nurse arrived with the boy's lunch just then so Sam left after promising to visit him again when he could. He went down to Reception to wait for Holly.

She came hurrying through the doors a short time later, her face lighting up when she saw him.

It seemed the most natural thing in the world to put his arm around her and kiss her, despite the amused looks they attracted from people passing. He didn't care. He wanted the whole world to know how he felt because he felt so wonderful!

'Benny's fine, you'll be glad to hear. Dad popped round to see him this morning. Peg gave him a real telling-off when she found out what he'd been up to,' Holly informed him as they drove back to Yewdale.

'I can imagine.' Sam laughed. 'I don't think Benny will be getting up to any mischief for a while, although I suspect it was Sean Jackson who was the instigator.'

'How did you guess? Evidently, it was Sean's idea that Jason should hide in the pottery. He knew about the faulty fire-escape door. Sean's been taking him food but they had to let Benny in on the secret when he saw them going in there one night.'

She slowed down as they reached the town. Sam stared curiously out of the window at the blackened building as they drove past. Most of the roof had fallen in so that it wasn't hard to imagine how lucky he'd been to escape so lightly.

'To think that you were in there…' She voiced his feelings, her green eyes full of fear as the memories surfaced.

'But I got out, sweetheart. And so did the others. It could have been a lot worse,' he said comfortingly, reaching over to squeeze her hand.

'Yes.' She took a determined breath then drove on. 'Anyway, young Sean wasn't the only member of the

Jackson family involved, as it turns out. The fire was started deliberately, and the finger is being pointed at Tracey's husband.'

'Really?' Sam couldn't hide his surprise. 'Why on earth would he want to do such a stupid thing?'

'Because he was furious that Tracey had got herself a job at the pottery and was going to stay here. Apparently, he'd been in there that morning and kicked up a fuss. Cyril Rogerson had him thrown out and he swore he'd get even. The police want to interview him.'

She drew up in front of the cottage. 'Shall I come in with you? Although perhaps you'd be better off going straight to bed.'

'If I told you that the answer to both questions is yes, what would you say?'

'That at least that bang on the head hasn't caused any lasting damage.' She leaned over to kiss him and her eyes promised him the whole world.

He kissed her back. 'I love you, Holly. Did I tell you that?'

'Oh, I think you mentioned it. However, don't people say that actions speak louder than words?' She got out of the car and came round to open the door for him.

'They do.' He grimaced as he levered himself awkwardly out of the seat, hampered by the fact that his arm was in a sling. A figure-of-eight bandage was keeping the broken ends of his clavicle together and would need to be worn for at least three weeks. 'Although I can't promise that the action will be all that effective.'

'Oh, don't worry about it, Dr O'Neill.' Holly took the key from him with a teasing smile. 'It's just another little problem which needs sorting out.'

CHAPTER TWELVE

MUSIC flowed up the stairs. Holly had put a record on when she'd gone down to make them something to eat. Sam smiled as he realised it was the one he'd played the last time she'd been there. He could never have imagined that things would work out like this back then!

'Right, here we are.' She came back with a tray and put it down on the side of the bed, frowning as she looked at the two plates. 'I certainly hope that the way to a man's heart isn't through his stomach, otherwise I may as well call it quits now.'

'It looks great,' he assured her, reaching over to steal a kiss. 'And you've already got my heart so there's no need to worry.'

'Good.' Holly passed him a plate and fork, laughing as he tried to juggle them one-handed. 'Can you manage?'

'Just about…' He forked up a mouthful of scrambled egg and ate it hungrily. 'Amazing how starving I am. Must be all the exercise.'

'Hmm,' she muttered, carefully avoiding his eyes as she picked up her own plate. Sam felt his heart turn over with sudden fear.

'You don't regret what happened, do you?' he asked huskily.

'No! Do you really need to ask?' There was a touch of colour in her cheeks as she looked at him. 'It was marvellous, Sam, everything I could have dreamed of. I'm just glad that I waited for the right man…for you.'

'Oh, darling!' He put his plate down and drew her to him, kissing her with a hungry urgency despite the hours they'd just spent making love. He sighed as he reluctantly let her go. 'Now we have to work out what we're going to do, don't we?'

'Yes. But before you say anything, Sam, I want to make it clear that I don't expect you to give up all your plans. I know how important it is to you, going to Africa, and I don't want you to decide not to go because of me and then regret it.'

Her voice was firm and determined. Sam smiled as he reached over and kissed her. 'How could I ever have thought you couldn't deal with this situation, darling?'

'Because at one time maybe I couldn't have handled it. But I love you, Sam, and all I want is for you to be happy.'

'And if I tell you that as long as I have you then I shall be? You are more important to me than anything else in the world, Holly.'

'I feel the same. But I know deep down that it isn't right for you to give up everything you've dreamed of doing,' she whispered huskily, brushing his mouth with a kiss that was just too tempting to resist.

Both of them were breathing a little harder after it was finished. Sam brushed the loose curls back from her face, marvelling at how much he loved her. He didn't want to think about being without her, but maybe there was a way around the situation. 'What would you say if I asked the agency if I could postpone my trip until after you finished at med. school?

Then we could both go out to Africa together to work.'

'Oh, Sam, would you do that? But do you think they'll agree?' She didn't try to hide her delight at the suggestion and his heart filled with joy.

'I'll get on to them straight away and see what they say. Are you sure it's what you want, sweetheart?'

'Of course it is. I can't imagine anything more wonderful than sharing your dream with you,' she said huskily. 'But if it can't be arranged, it won't make any difference to how I feel.'

'So you think you'll still love me at the end of two years, do you?' he teased, already sure of her answer.

'Two years, two decades, two lifetimes—I shall always love you, Sam. I don't want us to be apart but it won't change how I feel.'

'Then I don't think we need to waste any more time worrying, do you?' His mouth found hers and suddenly all the problems dissolved. All they needed to make things work was their love…

Sam drew the car to a halt but it was a moment before he got out. In the weeks since the explosion autumn had arrived and the trees on the nearby mountains blazed red and gold in the morning light. He'd never expected to be in Yewdale at this time of the year, but the agency had agreed to let him postpone his trip when he'd explained the situation to them.

It had caused less upset than he'd feared in the event because the doctor he'd been due to replace had been desperate to extend his stay in Africa to complete a project he'd been working on. It meant that everyone was happy with the new arrangements.

In the meantime, Sam would stay on in Yewdale, much to everyone's delight. Holly was back in medical school but she was due in Yewdale that night and he was looking forward to seeing her as he had something important planned.

Even David seemed to have accepted the situation and was happy for them. It was odd how well things were working out, considering how complicated they had appeared. Maybe being in love ironed out all the bumps!

He got out of the car to knock on the farmhouse door. The results of Helen Walsh's MRI had come back the day before but Sam hadn't wanted to break the news by phone. He'd called her that morning and had asked if he could come round so he knew that Helen would be expecting him. He smiled as she opened the door, thinking how much better she looked than the last time he'd seen her.

'Good morning, Helen. I hope it didn't put you out, calling round here?'

'Of course not. Come in, Dr O'Neill.' She led the way to the kitchen where Harvey was drinking a cup of tea. 'Sit down. I suppose this is about those tests I had.'

'It is,' Sam agreed as he sat down. He'd thought long and hard about how to tell her the news but it still wasn't easy.

'Let's hear it then, Doctor.' Harvey reached for his wife's hand and held it tightly.

'There's reason to believe that Helen has multiple sclerosis. The MRI showed patchy areas of damage to the white matter in the brain, which is a strong indication that the disease is present.'

'I…I thought it was a brain tumour like Mum's…' Helen sat down abruptly and put her hand over her mouth.

'Shh, love. It's all right, now.' Harvey looked sadly at Sam. 'What does it mean for Helen? Is she going to get worse and not be able to walk?'

'Not necessarily.' Sam saw their surprise. While he didn't intend to downplay the seriousness of the condition, he didn't want them to think that there was no hope. 'MS is caused by damage to the protective coverings of the nerve fibres in the brain and spinal cord. It occurs in patches so that some nerves can't carry impulses while others remain unaffected. Although MS is usually progressive it doesn't follow set patterns. A lot of people suffer symptoms like Helen has had recently, followed by long periods when they're perfectly fit. How do you feel at the moment, Helen?'

'Fine. Better than I've felt for ages, in fact.' She took a deep breath. 'Does that mean that it might have gone away for a while?'

'It's very likely. Nobody knows what causes MS but both physical and emotional stress can precipitate attacks,' Sam explained gently.

'Well, she's had plenty of both lately.' Harvey's tone was gruff. 'Helen told me about her dad. I could hardly believe she thought I'd behave that way. I told her that no matter what was wrong with her we'd get through it together.'

'And that's just the sort of attitude which will help Helen through this. You have to be positive about the disease and not let it rule your life. Do everything you want to as long as it doesn't overtire you. There are drugs which can help the more distressing symptoms if and when they occur. And there are trials going on to assess the value of Interferon, which is thought to slow the progress of the disease. That is something we shall have to consider.'

'Then it doesn't necessarily mean that I'll end up completely disabled?' Helen queried. Sam knew that it must be difficult taking it all in but she was handling it extremely well.

'Not at all. You could be perfectly well for months, maybe even years. Take things one day at a time, Helen. That's the best advice I can give you.' He got up, realising that they'd need time to talk this through.

'Make an appointment to see me, Helen, so we can discuss your treatment. A lot of people find a change of diet helps and that taking evening primrose or sunflower oils can be invaluable supplements. And if there's anything, no matter how small, you want to know then ring me. Promise?'

'I shall.' Helen got up and gave him a quick hug. 'Thank you, Dr O'Neill. I think the worst thing of all was being afraid. It's not half so bad now that I know what I'm dealing with.'

Sam drove back to Yewdale, glad that the Walshes had been so positive. But, then, it was always better to face the truth, as he'd found out for himself.

The day seemed to drag unbearably, mainly because he kept watching the clock. When Eileen buzzed to tell him Holly had arrived he felt his heart lift. His last patient had just left so he wasted no time in gathering up his things. She was outside the front door, talking to Abbie, but she broke off the moment she saw him.

'Hi, there.'

'Hi, yourself,' he replied, grinning inanely. He didn't even notice Abbie slipping away as he drew Holly into his arms. 'Have I told you that I love you lately?'

'Hmm, I'm not sure.' She smiled up at him with eyes full of love. 'Maybe you should tell me again, Sam, in case I forget.'

'Don't you dare!' He kissed her quickly then glanced over his shoulder as a patient came out of the door. 'I think we should find somewhere else to do this, don't you?'

'Afraid it might ruin your reputation, Dr O'Neill?' she teased. 'Isn't it a bit late to worry about that?'

'Oh, getting cheeky now, are you, young lady?' he growled, grasping her hand and pulling her after him as he marched towards his car.

He opened the door then kissed her lingeringly. Drawing back, he looked deep into her eyes. 'But you could be right. I wouldn't like the people in this town to get the wrong idea about my intentions.'

'So, what are your intentions, Sam?' She was still smiling as he reached into his pocket and drew out a small velvet-covered box. He heard her gasp as he opened the lid and she saw the ring nestling in the folds of satin. He'd spent ages looking, but as soon as he'd seen the ring in the window of an antique shop he'd known it was the right one. The emerald was the exact colour of her eyes, an exquisite square-cut stone surrounded by tiny diamonds set in a delicate gold band.

'I think this sums them up. I want everyone to

know how I feel about you, my darling—that you are the single most precious thing in my life,' he said softly.

'Oh, Sam! It's so beautiful. I can't believe that you found anything so perfect.'

He slipped it onto her finger then kissed her again. 'And I can't believe that I found you. I love you, Holly Ross, with my heart and my soul and everything I am. And one day in the not too distant future maybe you'll marry me.'

She kissed him back, her eyes adoring him. 'I love you too, Sam O'Neill. And there's no maybe about it. I have every intention of marrying you!'

He laughed as she slid into the seat. 'That's one promise I shall hold you to!'

'Right, has everyone got a glass?'

Sam looked around at the assembled throng as David called for order. The party hadn't been planned. David and Laura had invited a few people round to celebrate their engagement and things had snowballed once word had spread. Most of the town seemed to be packed into the house and the noise was tremendous. However, everyone grew silent as David held up his glass.

'I want you to join with me in offering Holly and Sam our congratulations and best wishes for the future—to Holly and Sam.'

The chorus rang around the room and Sam laughed as he acknowledged everyone's good wishes. He kissed Holly on the lips as they all clapped. 'I love you,' he whispered to her.

'I love you too.'

'How about us sneaking out of here?' he suggested. 'It seems ages since I had you all to myself.'

'Oh, at least an hour,' she teased.

'And that's far too long.' He took hold of her hand but she shook her head.

'Not yet.'

'You're not going off me already?' he demanded, pretending to glare. 'The champagne hasn't even had time to go flat yet.'

'No, I've not gone off you. I won't ever do that.' She reached up and kissed him. Turning away, she gave Laura a little wave and smiled when the older woman gave her the thumbs-up sign.

'What's going on?' Sam asked, frowning as he watched Laura walk over to stand beside David.

'Wait and see.' That was all Holly would say but he could tell that she knew.

'Ladies and gentlemen, I hope you'll bear with me while I propose another toast.' Laura claimed everyone's attention, including David's. Sam saw him frown as he turned to look enquiringly at his wife. It was obvious that David wasn't in on the secret, whatever it was.

A hush ran around the room as Laura raised her glass. 'It's probably a little early to wet the baby's head because he or she isn't due until May, but I can't think of a better time to make the announcement. Congratulations, David, darling, you're going to be a father again!'

'Did you know?' Sam demanded as a cheer went up.

'Yes. Laura told me this morning. It's brilliant news, isn't it? I just hope that Dad doesn't keel over from shock, though,' she added with a laugh as she looked at her father, who appeared stunned by the news. Everyone laughed when he gave a sudden whoop of delight, pulled Laura to him and kissed her soundly.

'Mmm, seems to be taking it very well so far,' Sam observed dryly. He watched as everyone surged forward to offer their best wishes, drawing Holly with him as he stepped out of the French windows. 'We'll congratulate them later. Now let's do a little celebrating of our own.'

The night was chilly but neither of them noticed it, wrapped up in each other's arms. Sam held Holly to him and his voice was suddenly husky. 'You do realise that could be us one day?'

'Celebrating because we're expecting a child?' She kissed him with loving tenderness. 'It's the ultimate commitment, Sam. Doesn't it scare you?'

'No.' He took a deep breath as his heart swelled. 'It doesn't scare me at all!'

EPILOGUE

THE party was still in full swing when Abbie slipped away. Nobody noticed her leave. They were all too caught up in the excitement.

She made her way back home, thinking about what had happened that night and how it made her feel. She was pleased for Sam and Holly, and thrilled for David and Laura, but she couldn't help feeling a little bit left out.

Everyone seemed to have found what they were looking for except her. Yet what was she looking for? Someone to love and love her in return, a family of her own? Was that what she wanted? Was she prepared to run the risk of being hurt again?

She sighed, realising that she didn't know what the answers were. She'd felt mixed up for some weeks now, ever since she'd heard about Nick Delaney's accident. She kept thinking about him and what had happened between them all those years ago…

She took a deep breath. That was all over and done with. She couldn't turn back the clock even if she wanted to. Nick Delaney was history!

* * * * *

Look out for Abbie's story next month in
THE HUSBAND SHE NEEDS
the final part of this exciting quartet.

COMING NEXT MONTH from 6th August

ONE IN A MILLION by Margaret Barker
Bundles of Joy

Sister Tessa Grainger remembered Max Forster when he arrived as consultant on her Obs and Gynae ward, for she'd babysat when his daughter Francesca was small. But Max wasn't the carefree man she'd known. Tessa wanted him to laugh again and—maybe—even love again...

POLICE SURGEON by Abigail Gordon

Dr Marcus Owen was happy to be a GP and Police Surgeon, until he found one of the practice partners was Caroline Croft, the woman he'd once loved. Caroline was equally dismayed, for she still loved Marcus! Brought back together by their children, where did they go from here?

IZZIE'S CHOICE by Maggie Kingsley

Sister Isabella Clark came back to discover a new broom A&E consultant, but being followed around by Ben Farrell ended with her speaking her mind and Ben apologised! Since he liked her "honesty", Izzie kept it up, but it wasn't until the hospital fête that they realised they might have something more...

THE HUSBAND SHE NEEDS by Jennifer Taylor
A Country Practice #4

When District Nurse Abbie Fraser hears that Nick Delaney is home, she isn't sure how she feels, for Nick is now in a wheelchair. Surely she can make Nick see he has a future? But at what cost to herself, when she realises she has never stopped loving him?

MILLS & BOON®

Next Month's Romance Titles

♡

Each month you can choose from a wide variety of romance novels from Mills & Boon®. Below are the new titles to look out for next month from the Presents...™ and Enchanted™ series.

Presents...™

A CONVENIENT BRIDEGROOM	Helen Bianchin
IRRESISTIBLE TEMPTATION	Sara Craven
THE BAD GIRL BRIDE	Jennifer Drew
MISTRESS FOR A NIGHT	Diana Hamilton
A TREACHEROUS SEDUCTION	Penny Jordan
ACCIDENTAL BABY	Kim Lawrence
THE BABY GAMBIT	Anne Mather
A MAN TO MARRY	Carole Mortimer

Enchanted™

KIDS INCLUDED!	Caroline Anderson
PARENTS WANTED!	Ruth Jean Dale
MAKING MR RIGHT	Val Daniels
A VERY PRIVATE MAN	Jane Donnelly
LAST-MINUTE BRIDEGROOM	Linda Miles
DR. DAD	Julianna Morris
DISCOVERING DAISY	Betty Neels
UNDERCOVER BACHELOR	Rebecca Winters

On sale from 6th August 1999

H1 9907

Available at most branches of WH Smith, Tesco, Asda, Martins, Borders, Easons, Volume One/James Thin and most good paperback bookshops

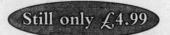

2 FREE

books and a surprise gift!

We would like to take this opportunity to thank you for reading this Mills & Boon® book by offering you the chance to take TWO more specially selected titles from the Medical Romance™ series absolutely FREE! We're also making this offer to introduce you to the benefits of the Reader Service™—

- ★ FREE home delivery
- ★ FREE gifts and competitions
- ★ FREE monthly Newsletter
- ★ Exclusive Reader Service discounts
- ★ Books available before they're in the shops

Accepting these FREE books and gift places you under no obligation to buy, you may cancel at any time, even after receiving your free shipment. Simply complete your details below and return the entire page to the address below. *You don't even need a stamp!*

YES! Please send me 2 free Medical Romance books and a surprise gift. I understand that unless you hear from me, I will receive 4 superb new titles every month for just £2.40 each, postage and packing free. I am under no obligation to purchase any books and may cancel my subscription at any time. The free books and gift will be mine to keep in any case.

M9EA

Ms/Mrs/Miss/Mr ....Initials.....................................

BLOCK CAPITALS PLEASE

Surname ....

Address ....

....

....Postcode....................................

Send this whole page to:
THE READER SERVICE, FREEPOST CN81, CROYDON, CR9 3WZ
(Eire readers please send coupon to: P.O. BOX 4546, DUBLIN 24.)

MILLS & BOON®

Makes any time special™

Bestselling themed romances brought back to you by popular demand

Each month By Request brings you three full-length novels in one beautiful volume featuring the best of the best.

So if you missed a favourite Romance the first time around, here is your chance to relive the magic from some of our most popular authors.

Look out for
Passion in August 1999
featuring Michelle Reid,
Miranda Lee and Susan Napier